ChupaCabra Meets Billy the Kid

CHICANA & CHICANO VISIONS OF THE AMÉRICAS

ChupaCabra Meets Billy the Kid

RUDOLFO ANAYA

UNIVERSITY OF OKLAHOMA PRESS : NORMAN

This book is a work of fiction. Names, characters, places, and incidents are either the product of the author's imagination or are used fictitiously, and any resemblance to actual events, locales, or persons, living or dead, is entirely coincidental.

Library of Congress Cataloging-in-Publication Data

Name: Anaya, Rudolfo A., author.
Title: ChupaCabra Meets Billy the Kid / Rudolfo Anaya.
Description: Norman, OK : University of Oklahoma Press [2018]
Series: Chicana & Chicano Visions of the Américas ; volume 21
Identifiers: LCCN 2018001380 | ISBN 978-0-8061-6072-6 (hardcover : alk. paper)
Classification: LCC PS3551.N27 C48 2018 | DDC 813/.54—dc23
LC record available at https://lccn.loc.gov/2018001380

ChupaCabra Meets Billy the Kid is Volume 21 in the Chicana & Chicano Visions of the Américas series.

The paper in this book meets the guidelines for permanence and durability of the Committee on Production Guidelines for Book Longevity of the Council on Library Resources, Inc. ∞

1 2 3 4 5 6 7 8 9 10

THE BALLAD OF BILLY THE KID
by Rudolfo Anaya

It was a dark and sad night
in the village of Fort Sumner,
when Sheriff Pat Garrett
Billy the Kid did kill,
Billy the Kid did kill.
Eighteen hundred and eighty-one,
how well I remember,
when in Pedro Maxwell's home
two fatal shots he fired,
two fatal shots he fired.

Fly, fly, gentle dove,
to the Río Pecos villages,
tell all the young women
that Billy is dead,
that Billy is dead.
Oh, what a coward Pat Garrett,
he didn't give Billy a chance!
In the arms of his love,
he killed him,
he killed him.

Oh, what sadness fills me
when I see Rosita crying,
and poor Billy in her arms,
with his blood flowing,
with his blood flowing.
Fly, fly, gentle dove,
to the Río Pecos villages,
tell all the young women
that Billy is dead,
that Billy is dead.

I completed the first draft of *ChupaCabra Meets Billy the Kid* in 2009. I had already published *Curse of the ChupaCabra*, which takes place in Los Angeles, and *ChupaCabra and the Roswell UFO*, which takes place in New Mexico.

Early in 2010 my wife died, and I turned my attention to writing *The Old Man's Love Story* and *The Sorrows of Young Alfonso*. I forgot the Billy the Kid novel until 2016. While searching in my computer for a children's story, I came upon the Billy the Kid file. I was surprised: the story had been waiting for me those seven years.

I sent the manuscript to my good friend Enrique Lamadrid. He gave it a close reading, made some valuable suggestions, and encouraged me to send it to my publisher. I went to work revising. That Christmas of 2016, my editor, Robert Con Davis-Undiano from the University of Oklahoma Press, was visiting here. He read the manuscript and enthusiastically said he wanted to publish it. I didn't think it was quite ready to submit, so once again I went to work revising.

When I thought the story was ready, I sent the final draft to Robert. He passed it on to Emily Jerman Schuster, an editor at OU Press. She really liked the story, and she was a great help in cleaning up my messy manuscript. After that, the story was sent to Jane Lyle, an excellent editor who had edited some of my previous works. I was delighted to have her as my editor again.

In November 2017, I spent the month reviewing Jane's comments and suggestions. She intimately knew Billy the Kid's history, so her editing was most helpful. During this time, my niece Belinda helped by going through my old files and verifying information that I needed. So much has been written about the life and times of Billy the Kid that I wanted to get dates, names, events, and places as correct as possible.

Is there a moral to the history of this book? I'll let the reader decide. I can only share the surprise and joy I felt when I came upon Billy's story, which had lain dormant so long in my computer. It still called to me, but it needed work. I got to work, writing day and night, helping this novel come to a new plane of life, a new birth. I am thankful for the encouragement and close readings others have offered, editing that obviously improved the story. Mistakes the reader may find in the book are mine alone.

—Rudolfo Anaya

ChupaCabra Meets Billy the Kid

"Some believe the Arrow of Time flies only from Now to the Future. What if it flies from the Past to Now?"

Marcy's note appeared on Rosa's laptop.

"What does that have to do with me?" Rosa typed back.

"In 1947 a UFO crashed near Roswell, New Mexico. In it, the U.S. Air Force found the body of an extraterrestrial. Some of the top generals organized a secret government agency called C-Force. Their scientists performed an autopsy on the alien."

"I know," Rosa replied. "Why do you keep coming back to the Roswell UFO?"

"Roswell is where the spaceship picked me up," Marcy wrote. She laughed, a faraway laugh that broke the silence in Rosa's room.

Rosa shivered. She had seen Marcy board a UFO and disappear into the vacuum of space that hung over Roswell early one March evening. Was Marcy living in the UFO as she claimed? She kept sending messages to that effect. But how was that possible?

Rosa felt a chill every time she got a note from Marcy. Why had she seemed so at peace with herself as she walked toward the UFO? Had she boarded a spaceship before?

Did UFOs visit from outer space? Where did they come from? Why are they interested in us? Marcy called the UFO argonauts our "brethren," our "relatives." "They watch over us," she said. "When humans get too out of hand, they will push a button, and *poof.* We'll have to start all over again."

"Back to the cave?" Rosa asked.

"Maybe further back, maybe to our origins in the Big Bang. Made from the organic dust of that galactic singularity."

Rosa stared at her laptop. Marcy said the Arrow of Time was real. Yes, thought Rosa, seasons come and go; we are born, live, and die. The hours move by, second by second on the clock, one after another.

Even if the face of a clock is round, time still flies away in a straight line. Or does it?

What is time, anyway? Why do we say it flies? Where does time disappear to? The Arrow of Time is the most powerful force in our lives. Once time is gone, you can't bring it back. But Marcy's comments—what did they mean? Was she suggesting that the past can appear in the present? She had told Rosa to check out Einstein's theory of relativity. He explained space-time, space and time being one force, a physical law most can't comprehend.

Space and time, time and space—Rosa mulled them. Have we existed in a foreign universe for a million years now? In another million years, will we live in the future? Tossed around by space-time, mere images? Here in the present, then in the past, then in the future, until the universe ends. Does the expanding universe have an end?

Rosa frowned. She had read Stephen Hawking's book, but the theories of that wizard remained a mystery. He understood the secrets of the universe. Black holes and dark energy were home to him. And so were supernovas. The explosion of a star had created a wormhole, he theorized, and one could enter the wormhole and travel to other dimensions at the speed of light.

Rosa shook her head. She heard Marcy laughing again. But if Marcy was on the UFO, why was she able to hear her?

There were other sounds in the dark night that hung over the Puerto de Luna Valley. The occasional screech of an owl, angry coyotes at the river yapping and snarling as they fought over a kill, a porcupine or badger. The rushing river, moving south with time. Shorty's horses whinnied in the corral next door. Someone was out there.

Rosa had taken the summer off to work on her novel about the famous New Mexican outlaw Billy the Kid. The village of Puerto de Luna on the Pecos River was the perfect place for her. It was quiet, and her neighbors, Shorty and Eloisa, had become good friends. Her grandparents had lived in the village years ago. She felt at peace in their querencia, the home they had constructed and lived in all their lives. Maybe it would become her home space.

"Crazy," she sputtered at the thought. She would never leave LA and her work at the rehab center. Too many kids depended on her.

She remembered her grandfather telling her witch stories. Long ago there was a case of witchcraft in the village. He had asked Ultima, a curandera, to come to Puerto de Luna to lift the curse. Rosa had read a novel about it when she was studying at the University of New Mexico.

Now, the deeper she got into Billy the Kid's life, the more other stories got tangled in her mind. Novels she had read kept jogging her thoughts as she wrote, poems from long ago, scenes from movies, all interfering. Staying focused on Billy's story was exhausting her.

The first few weeks had been like a vacation. In the mornings, she wrote; in the afternoons, she borrowed Shorty's mare, Mancita, and rode along the river and into the hills. She returned refreshed to work at night, but lately she realized she wasn't getting to the heart of the story. She didn't really know her character. Who was the real Billy the Kid?

She had read every book written about him, and she had interviewed old-timers who remembered stories their grandparents told. There were bits and pieces of his life here and there, a few yellowed letters, a lost manuscript. There were still a few around who claimed to be his descendants. Some talked of exhuming Billy to get his DNA, hoping theirs would match his.

She had shared a lot of this information with her friend CiCi, who was also working on a book about Billy the Kid. Questions had come up: What if Billy wasn't buried in the Fort Sumner cemetery? And what about the old man in Texas who for years had claimed he was the Kid? Everyone had a story to tell.

Rosa understood that everything she had read about Billy didn't make a novel. A novel exposed life through the imagination of the author. *Don Quijote* informed readers about the Spanish customs of the time, but the real story was about the man. He was a character created larger than life by his author. The story had been read and analyzed for centuries, and would be for many more.

Writers always hope their characters will live beyond them. That will imbue the author with a kind of immortality. That is, as long as the book is still around. All the books in the ancient Library of Alexandria had been destroyed. Also those in the library at Ephesus. But what about digital libraries? Was the cloud invincible?

"Damn!" Rosa cursed. The real Billy was missing in her story, and she knew it.

She stopped riding in the afternoons and began to work from morning till midnight. She stopped visiting her neighbors. The story consumed her; and worse, she knew she still wasn't getting at the truth. She felt the need to be there, in Billy's time, to know every-thing. But that was impossible.

She returned to her message to Marcy. "Hope I'm not losing it," she typed. Is *time* simply a human invention? Everything and every-one always moving forward, never backward. And what did forward mean? Gravitational waves curve space-time. Could gravity curve the Arrow of Time? Or the other way around?

Space-time was some kind of continuous web into which the universe was molded. Did the Big Bang create space-time? Are there multiple universes or only the one? One billion stars in this galaxy, another billion over there. Somewhere.

"What would you give to get at the truth of Billy's life?" Marcy's question appeared on the laptop screen.

"Everything," Rosa replied.

"Your soul?"

"Is this a bargain with the devil?"

"Take it or leave it."

"Yes. I want his story to ring true. I want the novel to reflect his time, the people, the places—not like all the phony stories written about him. Or those stupid Hollywood movies."

"I can arrange that," Marcy said. "I can take you there."

"Not possible!" Rosa typed angrily. "You're dead. Gone with the UFO."

Marcy laughed. "Not gone—hovering above Earth with my brethren. I know the life of Billy the Kid forward and backward. Remember, I was the Roswell librarian. I collected and read everything ever written about him."

"Help me," Rosa typed. "I want to know the real Billy. How do I get the truth?"

"Through a wormhole," Marcy said.

"What?"

"Yes. You can travel to Billy's time through a wormhole."

"Actually be there?"

"Yes, experience everything firsthand."

"Not possible. You're messing with my mind."

"You said you would give everything."

"Yes, to get the story right I will. I will sell my soul. Take me there!"

"Deal!"

Rosa's laptop shook slightly. She glanced at the clock. It was past midnight, and she was dead tired. She folded her arms on the desk, laid her head on them, and closed her eyes. She had been writing all day, and she had the awful feeling that comes with falling out of the zone, that creative time when a writer feels truly connected to the story in process. Billy's real story was evading her. She wasn't getting to the truth.

"You ready?"

"Yes." Rosa groaned and looked up. Light from the lamp reflected off the flash drive on the desk. She wondered if this was part of her problem—why she couldn't get to the real Billy. Marcy had given the small device to her to safeguard. According to Marcy, it contained the genomes of ChupaCabra and the space alien, the extraterrestrial that had been recovered from the UFO crash site by C-Force. An autopsy had been performed on the alien. Half the world had seen the video of it. Half the world believed it was real.

Marcy had hacked the C-Force computers and stored the genome formulas on the flash drive. C-Force scientists had recovered enough alien DNA to construct the Roswell alien's genome. They had also finalized the genome of the creature known as ChupaCabra.

Genome characters floated in Rosa's mind. Strange stuff that meant absolutely nothing to her. If Marcy was telling the truth about what the flash drive contained, it was extremely valuable. Scientists would use the information to learn more about extraterrestrials and the elusive ChupaCabra.

But C-Force had more nefarious motives in mind, Marcy had warned her. C-Force scientists had combined the DNA of the alien with that of ChupaCabra in an early experiment. They had created the first four copies of a new type of ChupaCabra called a Himit. The most dangerous of these, the main Himit, was the one they called Saytir. Saytir possessed strange and super powers. Unlike the other three Himits, he could not be killed. And Saytir could morph.

"C-Force reports only to the president," Marcy said. "With the genome formulas, he's crazy enough to create a monstrous army of Himits."

"To rule the world?"

"What every dictator dreams of."

That's why Nadine had driven her car loaded with plastic explosives into the C-Force laboratory in Roswell. Saytir and everything in the building had gone up in a gigantic explosion.

Rosa heard a noise, shivered, and looked up. Outside a breeze moaned in the hot July night. Behind her house, the Pecos River cut a path through the Puerto de Luna Valley. Her ancestors had farmed the valley, planting apple orchards, fields of corn and chile, and vegetable gardens. People from as far away as Alburquerque swore that Puerto de Luna chile was the best in the state.

She cocked her head and listened to the gurgle of the river blending with the constant song of summer crickets. Outside an owl cried, and Rosa stiffened. "Relax," she told herself. Saytir and his mad scientists were incinerated in the explosion.

"Not true," Marcy wrote. "Saytir didn't die, and he wants the flash drive. Guard it with your life. Time to go."

Rosa heard a horse whinny. In the corral, Mancita snorted in greeting. Someone was outside. Her neighbors never came to visit this late. She walked to the door, opened it, and peered into the dark.

A tall, slim cowboy alighted from a lathered pony. "Buenas noches," he said in greeting.

"¿Quién eres?" Rosa asked.

"I'm William Bonney," the cowboy answered. He stood in the light cast from the room.

Rosa smiled. The young man had just said he was Billy the Kid. She studied him carefully. He *did* resemble the image in the well-known photograph that showed the Kid standing, pistol in a holster, a Winchester rifle held in one hand, a well-worn sombrero on his head, a slightly crooked smile, buckteeth.

Not possible, Rosa thought. Not William Bonney alias Billy the Kid, the subject of my novel. Am I dreaming? Or hallucinating?

"Who are you?" she asked again.

"Folks down in Lincoln County call me Billy the Kid," he said and stepped forward.

2

"What do you want?" Rosa asked, wondering who really was standing in the light of the open door. Billy the Kid, as he claimed, or an imposter?

She thought of the gun in her desk drawer. Bobby, her fiancé, had visited early in the summer and brought her a small-caliber pistol. For protection, he told her. They had practiced shooting targets at the river. She knew he worried. Rosa had tangled with ChupaCabra in Roswell, and before that aboard a cruise ship sailing to Los Angeles. Bobby, an LA detective, had access to a lot of government information, but C-Force's existence was clouded in secrecy. He could find nothing: every file had been deleted.

"Why?" Rosa asked Marcy.

"I told you. C-Force has moved into the Oval Office. The president and his close advisor now control C-Force. Lord help us if they get hold of the flash drive."

"Why give it to me?" Rosa wrote. "You double-crossed me!"

"Excuse me," the cowboy said. "Din't mean to upset you."

"You didn't," Rosa said, pointing at the laptop. "Marcy did."

"That's some marvelous machine. You write on it?"

"Yes. But why are you here?"

"I'm here to help you."

"How the hell can you be *here!*" Rosa exploded.

Billy the Kid had been dead since 1881. Sentenced to hang for the 1878 murder of Lincoln County sheriff William J. Brady, he had escaped from jail in April 1881, killing two deputies in the process. Two months later, he himself was killed by the sheriff of Lincoln County, Pat Garrett. And yet the man now standing in front of Rosa, offering his help to her, claimed to be the Kid. And he was carrying a pistol and rifle, so what did he mean, *help?*

"Who are you?"

"I tol' you, I'm William Bonney. The vaqueros down in Lincoln County call me the Kid. I'm here to—"

"I don't believe you!" Rosa cut in.

Billy shrugged. "I came fast as I could."

Ridiculous, thought Rosa. I'm not going to stand here and argue with someone who claims to be Billy the Kid. She peered into the cowboy's eyes and drew a deep breath. Could it be?

"Din't Marcy tell you? Saytir isn't dead. He's coming for this thing you have." He pointed to the flash drive on the desk.

"The flash drive?"

"Yup. Whatever that is."

"Saytir died in the Roswell explosion."

"Not true. Saytir tricked Nadine. Marcy said Nadine should've known better. He used a Himit as a double, an' Himits can be killed. But not Saytir."

Rosa nodded. Yes, she knew about the Saytir clones, the ones Nadine had called Himits. Saytir was the most powerful Himit created by C-Force. Saytir was ChupaCabra.

"How do you know all this?"

"Marcy."

"You heard her?"

"Yes, she communicated with me. Maybe it was a dream, but it was so clear, like she was standin' next to me. An' she said Saytir is out to get you. He wants that thing. Din't she tell you?"

"Stay put!" Rosa stepped back and read Marcy's message.

"You said you wanted the real story. Here it is. You made a deal, now you have to go with him. You're caught in the Arrow of Time."

Rosa typed back, "This is crazy. How did he get here?"

"A wormhole."

"What?"

"A wormhole opened up along the river. Perhaps it's always been there. You remember the stories our grandparents used to tell about witches, how they could turn into owls and fly around. Maybe they just used wormholes to get from one place to another."

"Ridiculous!" Rosa shouted at the laptop.

Rosa heard Marcy laugh. "Maybe. Anyway, now it's your turn. You're going to Billy's time."

Rosa's hands shook as she typed, "I don't believe you." She glanced at the cowboy, who waited patiently at the door. "Why me?"

"You wanted to go there. You made a deal, right?"

Rosa looked at the pile of papers on her desk: her manuscript, *The True Story of El Bilito*. Yes, she had been working like hell to get the story to come to life, but it just wasn't happening.

"By writing the story, you got into Billy's time. Isn't that what writers do, get so deep in the story they feel like they *are* in the story? The author becomes a character, and the character is trapped. You're not quite there, are you? You haven't captured the Arrow of Time."

Rosa shrugged. She had gone as far as she could into Billy's life, but something was missing. She needed to feel and breathe Billy's life. Touch and see the people in his life, hear their voices.

Is that why he was standing at her door? Was he an apparition? A fiction of her imagination gone wild? Could she capture the Arrow of Time?

"Why is he here?"

"There's danger to him, and to you if you don't get the story right," Marcy answered. "You're only halfway there."

"I don't understand."

"Billy came through the wormhole. You have to follow him, finish telling his story, the true story. You need to go through the wormhole to get to Billy's world."

"To get to know the real Billy? To construct his world in *my* novel?"

"Yes. It's like love, isn't it? It *is* love. You love Billy, your main character. He loves you back and wants to help. That's why he came."

"I . . . I don't have to go."

"The only way to know the real story of your Bilito is to go with him. Saddle up. This is a great opportunity."

"This is all make-believe," Rosa typed. "I'm not Dorothy! There is no rabbit hole!"

"Only a wormhole," Marcy typed back. "It's your ticket to a marvelous reality. Guard the flash drive. Billy will help."

"Saytir wants it."

"Yes."

Getting tangled up with ChupaCabra at Roswell had led her down this strange path. Nothing made sense anymore.

"Am I neurotic?"

"No, just in love with Billy. What a tangled web authors weave when they fall in love with their characters."

"So now I'm Spider-Woman," Rosa said sarcastically. "Weaving a story?"

"Good metaphor," Marcy replied. "Writers aspire to be God-like. Create a universe in the stories they write. Go with Billy and learn all you can. Then maybe you can bend the Arrow of Time into your story."

Rosa turned and looked at Billy. "So you're Billy the Kid?"

"Yup. Marcy said you got to go with me."

It's all in my imagination, Rosa thought, trying to rationalize what was happening.

Billy smiled. "You're writin' my story. Safe behind your desk. Now you have to go with me. Get your hands dirty, ride with my amigos, the Regulators. Meet my friends Martín an' Josefa."

"Why?"

"You made a deal, got to keep it. Be witness to my true history. I guess that's what a writer does, isn't it? Be witness, like in church. Anyway, we've got to get away from Saytir. We've got to go."

"Where?"

"Down to Lincoln County. That's where most of my story takes place. Marcy tol' me a lot, but not everything. I know about the ChupaCabra you met on a ship, an' about you and Nadine in Roswell."

Rosa had met Nadine in Santa Fe, and together they had driven to Roswell. Nadine's motive was to destroy C-Force. The trunk of her car was loaded with explosives.

"Did Marcy tell you about wormholes?"

"Nope. I know a little science, an' less Greek." He smiled.

"In a wormhole, a person can go from one dimension to another. The Arrow of Time curves. It has to do with string theory. The universe is composed of taut electromagnetic strings. When they vibrate, they set off ripples . . ." She stopped. "It doesn't make sense, does it?"

"Nope."

Rosa slumped into the chair. Electromagnetic strings? Butterflies? Gravitational waves moving across the universe? Dark matter? What else, she thought. Space-time rules the universe. Or is it gravity? Or the dark energy Hawking wrote about?

"You have to control the Arrow of Time," Marcy wrote. "Your love for Billy is step one. But the Arrow has to be captured in your novel."

"I know C-Force created Saytir," Billy said. "Also some other smaller Himits. That's what Marcy said. But we don' have time. We've gotta get goin'."

"Where?"

"Back to Lincoln County. Listen!"

Something was moving outside. Billy stepped in front of Rosa. "The thing followed me here," he whispered.

"What thing?"

"A Himit."

A cowboy appeared at the door, green face and eyes of fire.

"ChupaCabra!" Rosa cried out.

"Stand back, cowboy," Billy ordered.

"Not till I get what I came for!" the Himit shouted. "The flash drive or your life!" He drew his pistol, but Billy was faster. He fired, and the bullet hit the Himit between his fiery eyes. Crying in pain, the monster turned and ran.

Down the road a dog barked, a door opened. Neighbors had heard the gunshot. That happened once in a while, someone scaring coyotes away from a chicken coop. After a few minutes, the door closed.

Billy holstered his pistol. "He won't go far," he said. "Drop by the time he gets to the river. You okay?"

Rosa nodded. In that split second, she became a believer. If Billy had not been there, the monster would have—she trembled at the thought. ChupaCabra had killed two of her students by piercing their skulls with its fangs and sucking out their brains. The Himits were equally as dangerous. They followed Saytir's orders.

"I guess I came in time," Billy said. "Saytir's out there. We've got to go."

"We should call the sheriff," Rosa blurted, and instantly realized her mistake. Call the local sheriff and say Billy the Kid had just killed a Himit? They would call her crazy.

"Cain't trust anyone. Git your stuff."

She had no choice. She had to follow Billy. She grabbed her back-pack and stuffed in her laptop, her solar charger, some pencils and paper, her notes, some energy bars. She put on a light jacket and put the flash drive in a pocket.

"I'm ready."

"You need a horse. The mare in the corral."

"We can't take that one. She belongs to Shorty López."

"Borrow it," Billy said in a stern voice.

"Yes. I'll write him a note." She grabbed a pad and started to write a note, but she couldn't tell him she was going to 1878 Lincoln County. It didn't make sense.

They walked out. In the moonlight, the village was dissolving. She rubbed her eyes. The cottonwood trees by the river were shimmering, creating illusion after illusion.

The river, she thought, the river. Her grandfather had told her often, "Trust the river. The river is life. Water is life."

She glanced back at the house she had rented for the summer, whispered a prayer to the Virgin Mary, then followed Billy to the corral.

3

"Shorty, I'm going to camp downriver. Don't worry, I have Mancita. Be back—"

She didn't know when. Would he believe the note, anyway, or send the police after her? The whole thing was crazy. Why was she doing it? To get the true story of Billy the Kid? To save the flash drive? Or, as Marcy said, because such an adventure comes along only once in a lifetime?

They rode out of Puerto de Luna, the small Pecos River village where Rosa was renting the hundred-year-old house where Padre Polaco once lived. She had planned to write, enjoy a quiet summer, talk to the old-timers who still remembered her grandparents. Now she was riding out of the village with Billy the Kid.

The Arrow of Time, she thought, seemed to bend in many ways. Did it bring lives from the past? A dumb question. Billy *was* from the past. They rode down the main road toward the bridge.

Up to now, the summer had been tranquil. She had done some writing, visited with Eloisa and Shorty, listened to Mozart in the evenings—no television—and mornings she rode Mancita. She and the young mare had quickly formed a friendship.

Bobby and the kids she had helped at a drug rehab in LA had visited in June. She enjoyed showing them around the village. They got a big kick out of riding Mancita. They went to Santa Fe and met her parents, then down to the town of Lincoln. Leonor and Mousey enjoyed what she told them about Billy. Leonor, especially, was taken by the story. "He was tough," she observed. "Not much different than those of us who live in the streets in LA."

Was the Code of the West still a way of life? Teenagers growing up without much guidance learned to take care of themselves, defended their gang, took revenge when one of their own was attacked. There were as many guns per capita in the big cities as there had been in Lincoln County in Billy's time.

Had nothing changed?

Most of Billy's life had been turbulent. Leonor and Mousey could relate to that. The turbulent times in which Billy lived were much like theirs. But using a gun to solve your problems is not the answer, Bobby had cautioned. As an LAPD detective, he knew firsthand that many kids chose to settle scores with guns. Dozens were dying in the streets because of drug wars.

Rosa wondered what Leonor and Mousey would learn from the Billy the Kid story. Learn that it was best for the law to solve social problems, or idolize Billy, who had solved his problems with a gun?

The old people of Puerto de Luna still told stories that had been handed down from their great-grandparents. Billy the Kid had visited the village, he had a girlfriend there, and once he had stolen Padre Polaco's horses. The village was alive with stories, an oral tradition that fired up Rosa's imagination and found its way into her novel.

But the early, pleasant times had vanished as she got deeper and deeper into the darkness of her obsession, writing day and night, exhausted, not stopping to eat.

"Why are you here?" she asked.

"Marcy sent me. That thing, the flash drive, what are you goin' to do with it?"

"I hadn't thought about it until tonight—"

"You better get rid of it."

"Why?"

"Long as you have it, Saytir will come for it."

The Himit Billy had shot was like the one Nadine had killed on the road to Roswell. It had dissolved into greenish juices, leaving behind the smoldering membrane of some kind of silicone or plastic. These were the Himits that were part extraterrestrial and part ChupaCabra. Experiments in DNA cloning gone bizarre. Dangerous to Rosa because C-Force wanted the flash drive.

"Know what I think?" Billy said. "You got to bury that thing where it will never be found."

"Get rid of it so not even science can use it?"

"Yup. Far as I know, the thing contains something evil, how to create ChupaCabra Himits to rule the world. So said Marcy. It's unnatural. Cain't say I'm much into religion, even tho' my sweet mother taught me Christian ways, but I don' see those monsters as part of God's plan."

Rosa agreed. But bury it? Where? Did it have something to do with Billy?

"It's up to you," Billy said as they approached the bridge. "I used to visit Puerto de Luna. I love this place. But change is in-ee-vitable, like the preacher said. Me, I like it the way it used to be."

"I know," Rosa whispered. She knew the Kid's chronology, but did she know the truth in his heart?

"I rode over this land. Used to come up here to see friends. They had great dances here. I loved the bailes. My momma taught me to dance. She was a graceful lady. I had a girl here. Truth is, I had more than one girl." He chuckled.

"Why did Marcy send you?"

"For one thing, I'm a good shot. Put a hole in that Himit, din't I? Killed twenty-one men, the *Police Gazette* wrote. That's a bunch of bull. New Mexico was my territory. I want to clear my name."

"That's why you came?"

"Yup. I started to get Marcy's messages in my head, tho' I never met her. Rosa can clear your name, she said. Write my true story. I din't kill no twenty-one men. Never did. I joined up with Tunstall cause I thought it was the right thing to do. He was a good, honest man."

"You fought against the Dolan gang."

"They was bloodsuckers. Dolan joined up with the politicians in Santa Fe to steal every bit of land they could from the Mexicans down in Lincoln County. And up in the Taos area, too. The Santa Fe Ring controlled politics in New Mexico. They wanted the Mexican land grants, the water rights, the mines, an' the army contracts. Supplying the U.S. Army with beef was big business. The army had to feed the soldiers at Fort Stanton. Had to feed the Mescaleros an' Navajos at Bosque Redondo. Lord, they punished those poor Navajos."

Rosa knew. In 1864 the U.S. Army had begun the removal of the Navajos from their native land in Arizona to Bosque Redondo, a reservation near Fort Sumner. Many died on the Long Walk. Many died in what amounted to a prison camp at Bosque Redondo.

"A terrible time," Billy said. "The Civil War ended, an' displaced soldiers from the South moved in to get a piece of the New Mexico Territory. Homesteaders. The rich politicians of the Santa Fe Ring got hol' of many Spanish and Mexican land grants. Lucien Maxwell got the biggest. Their names are in the history books. The Mexicans was the underdogs. They treated me right. I learned to speak Spanish, so I threw in to hep 'em."

Rosa knew the history. Most of the stories written about Billy the Kid called him a vicious killer. Those stories sold dime novels and newspapers, but they didn't present the broader picture. In 1848, after the war with Mexico ended, the United States had taken a big chunk of Mexico's northern territories.

It is our manifest destiny to rule this land, President Polk had proclaimed. American businessmen and entrepreneurs migrated to the New Mexico Territory. The dishonest stole all the land they could get their hands on. They believed it was their manifest right.

"The politicians were on Dolan's side," Rosa said.

"Yup. The Mescalero Apaches were still roamin' the land. A small gang of them killed a few whites. Gave the president the excuse to send in the army. The real crooks were the land grabbers who took land from the Mexican farmers. Yes, I killed, an' there warn't anything good about that. An' I'm payin' for it. But most of the time there was a gunfight, newspapers wrote I was the one that did the killin'. Even if I warn't there. For one thing, I rode in late the day Jimmy Carlyle was kilt. He was already dead, but they pinned it on me. Governor Wallace put a price on my head."

They had reached the bridge. Rosa was surprised to see a row of lanterns lighting up part of the bridge, and a man on horseback right in the middle.

"We come too late," Billy whispered.

"Who's that?" she asked.

"Saytir."

4

"Who?"

The lanterns shone on a man on horseback in the middle of the bridge. They illuminated his holstered pistol, the sheriff's badge shining on his chest, and his white Stetson hat.

"It's the sheriff," Rosa said with relief.

"Saytir," Billy cautioned.

Had she heard right? Billy said Saytir. No, it was the sheriff.

"A Himit, alright. The old Apaches down Lincoln way called them shapeshifters. Witches who can change into owls, coyotes, even balls of fire. Wise old Apache tol' me a witch can spit a pebble into a man an' make him sick. I believe it. This one all dressed up as a sheriff is Saytir."

"But Saytir died in Roswell," Rosa insisted.

"No, this is Saytir, alright. Loves to dress up in different costumes. Tonight he's pretendin' to be the law."

"Hello, Billy," the sheriff called out as they approached. "Been a while."

"Hello, Pat," Billy answered.

"Pat Garrett?" Rosa whispered. The man who shot Billy in Fort Sumner on July 14, 1881? Not believable! But what was? She had seen a photograph of Pat Garrett. There was a resemblance, and now he greeted Billy as if they were long-lost friends. Indeed, back in Fort Sumner days, Billy and Garrett had been friends, gambled at cards together, and a few times probably rustled a few steers from John Chisum.

"Hello, Rosa," Garrett said, tipping his hat. "Been looking for you. See you're running with an outlaw." He leaned back and laughed.

Rosa's stomach churned. It was Saytir! But why in the role of Pat Garrett?

"Role-playing," Garrett chuckled. "Kids call it morphing. Didn't your friend Marcy tell you? I love role-playing. I get it from watching western movies. John Wayne and others. When those C-Force scientists created me, they did a super job. Super-Transformer! More dangerous than Terminator!"

He laughed again, a devilish chuckle that rolled down the river and made La Llorona stop and listen. Only a ChupaCabra could laugh like that.

Movies, Rosa thought. Scenes from movies exploded in her brain. Holograms, scenes from novels she had read. A boy ran across the bridge. "It's the Vitamin Kid," someone called. By the river pool below, Tony, Horse, and Bones were fishing for catfish. Farther down the river, La Llorona ran toward the boys, gnashing her pointed teeth.

"Holy moly! La Llorona!"

"Run, Tony, run!"

The boys ran, dissolving from Rosa's view.

It was like that. Since she had started writing, entire novels she had once read passed before her eyes. Shakespearean sonnets, passages from *The Divine Comedy*, the Bible, stories by Chicana writers she admired. They all clamored for attention, each wanting Rosa to review her latest novel. Their names spilled out of her subconscious like pearls.

She heard a symphony in the night air. Why? Was the Puerto de Luna Valley sacred space that could channel a person's past? A creative space? Or had she been infected by C-Force? Were they using her?

The hologram disappeared; she was back on the bridge.

"High noon," Garrett said. "Ain't this great. Me, you, and Billy standing on the Puerto de Luna Bridge over the Pecos River. The Old West. Billy as hisself and me as Pat Garrett. It had to come to this, Billy boy."

"Fine with me," Billy answered.

"Yes siree, so we meet here. You know, the Arrow of Time can propel us from there to here, from future to present and back to the past. Here time stands still. You know, this bridge was made famous in many a story. Lots of stories. In your grandparents' time, Rosa, a posse of penitentes once hung a woman accused of witchcraft here. Pushed her over the side, but the rope broke and she fell safe into the river. The good lariat of a cowboy don't break like that. That rope could hold a four-hundred-pound bull. You know what happened?"

"I expect she became La Llorona," Billy answered, "the crying woman who haunts the river."

Beneath the bridge, Tony, Bones, and Horse taunted La Llorona as they ran for their lives. "Help, murder, police! La Llorona fell in the grease!"

Garrett slapped his thigh and chuckled anew. "You hit the nail on the head, Billy. These old Hispanos will make a story out of the smallest incident. It's in their blood. A boy saw a golden carp in the Blue Hole. As a man he wrote the story 'bout the fish and the curandera Ultima. Hell, people have gotten too finicky. Feel sick, run to a doctor. In the old days, every Mexican woman knew how to mend a bullet wound and a broken heart. Ain't that right, Billy?"

"It's God's truth," Billy replied.

Garrett turned his attention to Rosa. "You've been holed up in Puerto de Luna writing stories, Rosa. History you call it. Writing Billy's history. Why bother, I already wrote it. *The Authentic Life of Billy the Kid*. Didn't I, Billy?"

"You left out a few details," an angry Rosa interrupted. "Like maybe you ambushed Billy!"

Garrett's eyes glowed red. He didn't like anyone poking around the fateful night he shot Billy. Hated those witnesses who swore he had bushwhacked Billy. All that could change right now. Get rid of Billy now, and he wouldn't have to kill him in Fort Sumner three years down the line.

Garrett's eyes flashed with anger. "You think you can find the truth after time has moved from there to here? There is no true history, just stories. Maybe you got caught up in your own story, Rosa. Now you're just a character in a dream. Stories are dreams."

Billy nudged his horse forward. "Bunch of nonsense, Pat. Just move on an' let us pass."

"You don't tell me what to do, Billy!" Garrett shot back.

Saytir would not take orders. He was ChupaCabra, the Himit who was more powerful than the rest. The scientists who had performed the early cloning experiments had put extra doses of DNA in Saytir, and God only knew what other steroids, genes, or hormones. Genetic therapy at its worst. They had created a powerful Terminator, one who could shapeshift.

"Grendel," Rosa whispered. The monster defeated by Beowulf. Poor Grendel's gone; a new Grendel has appeared, the troll on the bridge. The story swirled in Rosa's mind. She struggled to regain her composure.

"We can have it out right here if you want," Garrett threatened. "No gunfight at the OK Corral, but a gunfight on the Puerto de Luna Bridge. A new story will be born. The old codgers here can take and bury you in that godforsaken Pastura cemetery where some Bonneys from the old clan are buried. Ramón Bonney is buried there. So are Santiago and Salomón Bonney. Those two were fine vaqueros. A horse broke Santiago's foot in pieces. He walked with a limp after that."

"I been to Pastura," Billy said. "Small village on the llano. Ramón Bonney lived there. He hep me."

"I knew Ramón Bonney," Garrett said. "Two brothers came from England, Henry and Jim Bonney. Enrique and Santiago, the Mexicans named them. Ramón is Santiago's son. Enrique went to live in La Junta de los Ríos, later moved up to the Mora Land Grant. Ramón's kids settled in Pastura. Ramón lived with them in his old age. Those Bonneys married Mexican women, learned to eat carne seca, chile, and beans scooped up with tortillas."

Rosa had read the genealogy. Some claimed the name Bonney was from the French, Bonné.

"Bonney is your alias, Billy," Garrett said. "You're not a true Bonney."

"I was running from the law after killing the bully Joe Grant. I left Silver City in a hurry. I was near dead-tired when I stopped at Pastura. Ramón took me in, fed me, gave me a place to stay. I took his name."

"Now half of this county claims relationship to you," Garrett said. "The Messicans loved you. 'Los Bilitos' they called your gang. Robin Hoods. Damn it! You were outlaws."

"You should know about outlawing," Billy replied. "'Nuf talk. Let us through."

"Or what? You'll call the sheriff?" Garrett laughed. "Cain't you see, the town's asleep."

"Dreaming," Rosa whispered, feeling the eerie silence.

"Yup. I put a potion in the drinking water. They'll wake up tomorrow just fine. Won't know what hit 'em. There may be some babies born nine months hence, but that's not my concern."

"I've been drinking the water!" Rosa exclaimed.

"Don't listen to him, Rosa. He makes up stories."

"An' Rosa is in story time," Garrett said, grinning. "You're writin' Billy's story, but your story hasn't stopped time. And sure enough, the one thing that can stop the Arrow of Time is a story. Or maybe true love. Yep, a story stops time, at least while the story is being told. For the moment. For the Now."

"Then?"

"Then the Arrow of Time moves on, time marches on, as the common folk say. From here to eternity."

"'Nuf philosophy, Pat," Billy interrupted. "Time to move on."

"You cain't order me!"

"Try me," Billy whispered, his eyes glistening in the moonlight.

"You cain't change history," Garrett said. "You've got to get to your meeting with me in Fort Sumner. All I came for is the flash drive. It's got the genome of me and the alien, and I need it. A matter of life or death, you might say. Epigenetics, the latest. Hand it over, Rosa."

"It ain't yours!" Billy protested.

Garrett drew his pistol and aimed it at Rosa. "It's mine, alright.

And I will kill for it. Hand it over."

"Don't shoot!" Rosa exclaimed. "You can have it!" She took a shiny object from her pocket and waved it in Garrett's face.

"Mine!" Garrett gloated, smacking his reptilian lips.

"Rosa, no!" Billy cried, whipping out his pistol.

"Here!" Rosa shouted. "Take it!"

"Hand it to me. No tricks!"

"It's yours!" Rosa said, and tossed the object over the side of the bridge.

"Damn!" Garrett cursed. With no hesitation, he jumped on the bridge railing and dove into the dark. Huge bat-like wings opened, allowing the shapeshifter to glide down.

5

"Vamoose!" Billy cried. He slapped Mancita's rump and spurred his horse. They bolted across the bridge, fleeing from Saytir.

Saytir is a new Cyborg, Marcy had told Rosa. A kind of Terminator, but far more dangerous than the comic book or movie character. Those were basically metal frames covered with a flesh-like membrane. Nanocomputers allowed them to talk, see, walk, move their fingers and legs with great dexterity, do almost everything a human can do. But they were machines. Saytir, on the other hand, is a monster created by genetic engineering, made from ChupaCabra muscles and the extraterrestrial's biomechatronic devices. And C-Force scientists found enough genes to edit and thus fabricate a murderous ChupaCabra. The fountain of evil had been found in a lab.

These were Rosa's thoughts as they raced along the river bank, leaving Saytir behind, but not the fear of the confrontation on the bridge. How was he able to appear as Pat Garrett? Because he can morph, Marcy had said. All of this was a terrifying kind of science fiction for Rosa.

What other genes slept in the human genome? What remained to be discovered? Genes to order your child's personality, cure cancer, diabetes, and Parkinson's? No more dementia? The public would cheer. Live to be two or three hundred years old? Were there other, darker messages encoded in the genome that shouldn't be tampered with? Were scientists playing God?

Was there a gene or a group of genes controlling memory? Could memories be awakened by manipulating that specific constellation of genes? Could the collective memory of humankind be opened, like opening a can of sardines? What dreadful images from the unconscious might come floating to the surface? Characters from mythology would appear: Beowulf, Ishtar, Adam, Eve, and the Snake, Quetzalcóatl, Hitler, Genghis Khan, Lucifer.

The vast DNA storehouse of acids and proteins also held the dreams of poets and prophets. Shakespeare's genes, allowing us to know the most intimate thoughts of the *real* Shakespeare. Beethoven, Tchaikovsky, Little Richard, Freddy Fender, the Beatles?

The thoughts troubled Rosa, but she couldn't stop them. If Saytir could appear in any disguise he chose, how could they be sure when it was him? What defense did they have?

Where would it end? The genes were now being traced, isolated. Their functions had begun to be known, but there was something else hidden in the human genome: the memory of humankind. Ghosts and images from a past so ancient that they could only be known as shadows in the myths of the tribes of the earth.

"You sacrificed the flash drive," panted Billy, pulling his horse to a stop and dismounting. "Need to rest the horses. And take some air ourselves." They led the horses to the river to drink.

"Role-playing," Rosa replied, also breathless, taking the flash drive from her pocket. It glowed with a bright aura in the dim light of the moon.

"You threw Saytir a bone!" Billy exclaimed.

"Lipstick," Rosa said.

Billy slapped his leg and laughed. "I shoulda known you're too smart to let Saytir get the best of you. You know somethin' about him, don' you?"

"In different forms he has appeared in the myths and legends of the world. Call the creature what you will, he's always been with us. Deep in our subconscious."

"A creature like ChupaCabra?"

"Yes," Rosa replied. "ChupaCabra as Saytir. Throughout history, many a man has sought invincible power."

"And C-Force sits in the president's office," whispered Billy. "That's bad news."

"That's the story I should be writing!" an agitated Rosa cried out. "I need to turn back!"

"You cain't, Rosa."

"It's a matter of life or death! I can warn the FBI about C-Force. Call the papers, let the people know!"

"Calm down, Rosa, you cain't go back."

"Why?"

"You're caught in the Arrow of Time."

"Your time?"

"It's what you wanted, warn't it?"

Rosa nodded. Yes, it was what she wanted, Billy's story, but what could she do about C-Force in the White House? Nothing if she couldn't go back. Maybe all of this was make-believe. Who would believe Marcy flying around in a UFO, and Billy guiding Rosa to Lincoln County? Or Saytir as Pat Garrett? And a flash drive holding the most important genome formulas in the world?

"Is this real?"

"What?" Billy asked.

"Just thinking," Rosa answered, staring at the rolling waters of the river. "Marcy said there was a lost colony of ChupaCabras hidden for millennia in the mountains of Puerto Rico. A kind of lost species, a branch of *Homo sapiens*. They tried to keep away from humans until their forests were cut down. Then they learned to eat goats and chickens, smelled beans and rice cooking in the villages."

"So they warn't killers at first?" Billy asked.

"I don't think so," Rosa replied. "Destroying their environment dragged them into our time. We forced them from a life of harmony, perhaps a timeless existence. C-Force recognized their incredible strength. Their genome was intact, probably similar to that of Adam and Eve. First man and woman, first primates. Genes so pure, they hold immense power."

"So we're the ones who caused their downfall."

Rosa recalled what Marcy had told her, that humans were an interesting experiment being observed by space aliens who followed the drama from their spaceships.

"I guess there is some good in us, and its opposite. Maybe it was the plan all along. We think we're progressing, going forward, the beginning was too innocent, so we invented the Arrow of Time. Thought we could control time. In a hurry to get *there*."

"Wherever there is," Billy mused. "Right now it's in Lincoln. Try to clear my name."

"And I'm part of the plan."

"That's what Marcy said. You could finish writin' my story, but it won't ring *true* till you ride with me."

"Yes," Rosa answered. She had made a deal with Marcy, and now she was caught up in Billy's story, his time. To get it right, she had to ride with him. Until July 14, 1881, the fateful day in Fort Sumner.

"As long as you have what they want, Saytir will be after you, bitin' at your soul, draggin' you down."

"I'll learn to fight. If only I could read the flash drive, use its information to defend myself."

"Saytir's too dangerous, Rosa." Billy's face showed concern.

"I know, but there's something more dangerous. It's what they represent. The Himits were manufactured in a lab, but they are also shadows of ourselves. Each one of us has that shadow inside; else how do we explain the evil in in this world?"

"So we turn to violence," Billy said. "I know 'bout that. Time got violent in territorial New Mexico, and I did what every other vaquero was doin'. By the time I was fifteen, I had strapped on a pistol. Now everybody carries a gun."

"Do we really progress as time moves on?"

"We can only do our part," Billy replied. "I want to clear my name, an' you want to know everything about my life. Write my soul into your book."

"Yes. And the part I didn't know about you meeting up with Ramón Bonney."

"I stayed with him awhile. A good man."

After Billy's death, a rumor spread that he had really been buried in the Pastura cemetery. After all, Ramón Bonney and his clan lay buried in the St. Helen Catholic Church cemetery there. What if the Mexicanos didn't bury Billy in Fort Sumner? What if they buried him in Pastura? What if the Arrow of Time had curved there?

In the slowly moving water of the river, Rosa heard hushed Mexicano voices in the Fort Sumner night. Women cried as they intoned the rosary. A story was being born. Billy the Kid had just been killed by Pat Garrett.

"There's no Bonneys here in Fort Sumner," a voice said.

"You're right, Paco. They're all buried over in Pastura."

"Pues, vamos. We bury him in Pastura so he can be with his people."

The voices faded, Rosa opened her eyes. Where is Billy really buried? she asked herself.

Some historians noted that there were several accounts of Billy's death in Fort Sumner on the fateful night. Paco Anaya wrote his memoir of the night the Kid was killed. Rosa had his book in her collection. Pat Garrett wrote his own account, and that's the story most read.

History was clouded. Sure, one could find details, but never the real truth. History was a story being written in space-time, circling the Territory of New Mexico, and one entry was as good as the other.

_____

6

They came upon a sheepherder's ramada and stopped to rest. Billy always carried carne seca and hardtack biscuits in his saddlebag, so seated around a friendly fire, they ate and drank cool water from the river.

Billy pointed at her laptop. "I reckon it's up to writers like you to make the story interesting. you know, put a little ex-a-ger-ation in it."

"Your story doesn't need that," Rosa said. "You are well known in New Mexico history."

"History? My dear mother taught me to read the Good Book. Later I read the dime novels an' the *Police Gazette*. After she died, I got out of Silver City an' headed to Lincoln. I let my momma down. She done her best, an' I took up the gun. Makes you wonder, is it just in our nature to turn out dumb, so even a nurturing mother's guidance cain't help us?"

"Don't know," Rosa whispered. Even if Billy had had the most caring of mothers, would his destiny have been different? Was everyone's destiny wrapped up in the Arrow of Time?

Overhead the Milky Way sparkled, a belt of stars, home to those whose ships flew throughout the galaxy. Star people. Had Marcy become one of them? Were there others who had been taken up in the starships of the brethren?

Soon after their meal, Billy fell asleep, using loose straw for a pillow. The night was warm and the sounds from the river cottonwoods soothing. Swallows darted down, skimming the water for a drink. In the bosque, doves sang their songs of love. Every few minutes a new creature appeared as dusk darkened, bats flitting overhead. Once in a while a coyote called, accenting nature's domain.

Saytir's legions could have struck, and Billy would have slept through the last galactic battle. He was dead tired.

Rosa opened her laptop. Might as well record the journey. "Marcy,

I'm with Billy. On our way to Lincoln. Says he needs to clear his name. What's happening?"

Shortly a response Rosa did not really expect appeared on the screen: "You're caught in the Arrow of Time, the time of the river, the river of your ancestors. How fortunate!"

"What does the river have to do with this? Get me home!"

"Can't. You made a deal. You wanted to know Billy's real story, so there you are. Imagine the stories you will tell your grandkids. You have to follow him to the end."

"How long?"

"Till the fateful day." The screen went blank.

"Damn you, Marcy," Rosa whispered. "I can't, I can't . . ."

Fatigue finally lulled Rosa to sleep. Plugged into the laptop, the flash drive glowed and gave off imperceptible vibrations, as if responding to messages from starships zipping overhead.

Days later they rode into Lincoln, a gathering of homes on the Río Bonito. The American homes were mostly frame houses, the Mexicano homes made of adobe.

The Arrow of Time is whacked, Rosa thought. Time is reversed. This is the Lincoln of Billy's time, 1878.

The Mexicanos had been farming and ranching the area before the arrival of the Americans. From photos Rosa had studied at the Santa Rosa library, she recognized the Ellis home, Sheriff Brady's, Juan Patrón's, the jail, the old courthouse, the Murphy-Dolan store, and the McSween place.

"Up ahead is Martín's home. His wife, Josefa, cooks the best chile con carne in the territory. She's as good with a rifle as she is with her skillet. She's like a mother to me."

"You hungry?" Rosa asked.

"I could eat coyote steak," Billy replied, smiling. "I 'm glad to be home, an' to have you ridin' with me."

"I still don't know how I *really* got here."

"The Puerto de Luna Bridge. It's a bridge to here."

Rosa didn't understand.

"I miss Josefa's food. Come on, let's see what she's cookin'."

Martín was sitting on a bench in front of the house, playing his violin and singing for three kids who sat on the ground listening.

¿De dónde, de dónde vienes?
¿Dónde te perdiste?
Tu mamá y tu papá
Han estado muy tristes.*

When he saw Rosa and Billy ride up, he shouted, "¡Bilito!"

"Buenas tardes, Martín," Billy called as they alighted.

"Niños, vayan a sus casas. This is Billy the Kid."

"Billy the Kid!" the children screamed and ran off, their dog trailing after them.

"¡Qué gusto me da!" Martín said, hugging Billy in a bear-like abrazo. "And your friend?"

"Rosa. She aims to ride with me."

"Rosa, a beautiful name," Martín said, welcoming her. "Come, I throw some hay for the horses. You maybe clean dust."

Billy led Rosa to the well, where he filled a big tub with fresh water. He went back to talk to Martín while Rosa washed away the trail dust. After she was done, Billy cleaned up.

"I feel human again," Rosa said. "Thank you, Martín."

"Nuestra casa es tu casa," Martín replied. "Now we go surprise Josefa." He threw the door open and called, "¡Josefa! ¡Mira! ¡Bilito!"

Josefa looked up from the wood-burning stove, where thick slices of meat sizzled in a large skillet, splattering grease. On the comal, tortillas were browning. There were potatoes fried to a golden brown in another skillet alongside a pot of beans. The aroma of home-cooked food filled the small kitchen.

---

*From where, from where do you come?
Where did you get lost?
Your mother and father
have been very sad.

Josefa threw her apron aside and rushed to Billy. "¡Bilito!" she cried, hugging him in a big embrace. "Where did you go? ¡Cómo estás, qué gusto! And this beautiful young woman?"

She winked at Martín. Billy had never brought a woman before.

"I'm fine," Billy said, laughing. "This is my friend Rosa. She's writin' my story."

"Writing your story? Muy bien. Welcome to our casa, Rosa. Come, sit. Time to eat."

They wanted to know all about Rosa. Was she his querida, a new woman in his life? Rosa tactfully let them know that she was only along to write Billy's story. To do that, she would need to ride with him. Both Martín and Josefa were surprised. A woman riding with Billy and his vaqueros? They loved Billy as a son, so it was easy for them to accept Rosa into their home.

When dinner was done, Martín reminded Billy that Sheriff Brady was looking for him. "Te busca el sharife," he said with worry in his voice.

"No le tengo miedo," Billy replied.

"Ay, you not even afraid of el diablo!" Josefa said, and everyone laughed.

Brady, thought Rosa. Billy was destined to kill the sheriff in a shootout. "You can't," she blurted out.

"¿Qué?" Josefa asked.

"Nada," Rosa answered. "Just thinking." She understood that she couldn't talk about events that had already happened, much less influence them. Am I dreaming? she asked herself. No, she wasn't dreaming. Everything felt real, but she couldn't reveal what she knew of the past. She was only a spectator in a story already written.

"She write about you," Josefa said. "Qué bonito. A friend of Bilito is our friend."

Josefa made Rosa feel at home. She fed them great quantities of food, which they washed down with coffee. Billy ate as if he hadn't eaten in years. After the meal, the conversation turned to Tunstall.

Martín said, "Pues, they killed Tunstall."

Billy nodded and explained to Rosa an event she already knew. "We was in charge of Mr. Tunstall's nine horses. Dolan claimed he came to get the horses, but that was plain bullshit. We was almost at the Ruidoso when my friend John Middleton saw Dolan's posse fire on Mr. Tunstall. Jesse Evans, Tom Hill, an' Billy Morton killed Tunstall. Bushwhacked him. It was plain murder, an' I aim to get my revenge. Mr. Tunstall was like a father to me, an' if this is war, so be it."

Rosa looked at Billy. His blue eyes had turned cold with determination. Nineteen and vowing revenge, like the kids in the gangs in LA, where she had recently taught. The death of a gang member called for revenge. The old Code of the West was alive in the LA streets and in streets all over the country: take the law into your own hands.

"Will it ever end?" she whispered.

"I'll get them before I die," Billy answered.

This was part of Billy's mission, to get Tunstall's murderers, and she was deep in the action. Finishing the meal, they went out back to the corral and talked while they brushed down the horses.

"You want revenge."

"Sheriff Brady had Mr. Tunstall killed. I aim to even the score."

"It's wrong, Billy."

"Not in Lincoln County. It's war."

"I want no part of it," Rosa said sternly.

"You got no choice," Billy answered. "Marcy said you're in my time now. I don' expect you to carry a gun, but you do have to ride with me an' my amigos. It's the deal."

"You said your mission was to clear your name, not revenge!"

"Marcy said to trust me, din't she?"

"Yes . . ."

"Then you got to go with me to the bitter end," Billy said. "You told Marcy you would. That's why you're here."

Why was she arguing? The die was cast. Not even the gods of Olympus could change Billy's destiny.

7

"Ese cabrón mató una borrega," Martín said, coming up behind them, bowlegged but stepping lightly and carrying a Winchester rifle.

"¿Quién?" Billy asked.

Martín motioned, and they followed him to an arroyo behind the house.

"Por Dios," he said as he bent to examine the bloodstains.

"Cougar maybe," Billy said.

"No," Martín answered, and pointed at the tracks. "It walks on big claws like the devil." In the mud the tracks were as large as a horse's.

"It comes from the mountain," he said, and nodded in the direction of Sierra Blanca.

Rosa studied the tracks carefully. They weren't claws, but five toes so closely webbed they looked like claws. "It has five toes," she whispered.

Martín looked at the footprints again and said, "Mira nomás. I was wrong. I saw a claw print, but it has five toes. You have good eyes." He looked perturbed.

"Have you ever seen it?" Billy asked.

"I saw it one night. Big like a giant man and full of hair. It kill a goat and take it up the mountain. The Mescaleros call it Kensah, el Patas Grandes."

"Big Feet?"

"Sí. Patas Grandes."

"Sasquatch," a surprised Rosa said. He was describing the creature from the Pacific North.

"I know that word," Martín said. "Long ago some natives come from the north, Canada, I think. Come to do ceremony with the Mescalero. They say Sa-quache. Now I think it come with them."

Is it possible? thought Rosa. Sasquatch here?

"What are you aimin' to do?" Billy asked.

"Patas Grandes kill my sheep and take it. Two goats last winter. Everyone is afraid. The tracks are fresh. Today I find Patas Grandes."

"I'll go with you," Billy offered.

"Me too," Rosa said. She wasn't going to be left out of the mystery. How would it play into Billy's story? she wondered.

Josefa packed a lunch. "Cuidado," she cautioned, and gave her blessing. "Que la Virgen los cuide."

They saddled up and rode out of the village. Lincoln was waking to its daily activities. Some of the neighbors knew Billy was in town, and today he was riding with Martín. A young woman rode with them. Was this one of his queridas? Did he know that Sheriff Brady was ready to arrest him the minute he saw him?

They rode up the Río Bonito, following the tracks of the bigfoot creature that for years had come down from the mountain to kill sheep and goats, and one time a calf. The Anglo ranchers attributed the killings to cougars or packs of coyotes. Or the tracks belonged to whoever was poaching sheep. A few of the ranchers had tried to find the culprit, with no success.

The Mexicanos told stories of creatures that appeared in the night, like El Coco, a kind of boogeyman, and La Llorona, the crying woman. Stories to scare children into good behavior. In the village, Patas Grandes had become another legend. The village drunk claimed he had seen El Coco and La Llorona dancing by the river, but he didn't want to meet up with Patas Grandes at night. What would one do if that happened?

"What do you think, Billy?"

"No sé."

"Has it ever killed a person?" Rosa asked Martín.

"No, it never attack anyone. Maybe it know we have the rifle. All my life I live here, ese animal never hurt any person."

"So why kill it?"

"I feel bad, but my sheep are my food. I eat or Patas Grandes eat."

Blue jays called, and ravens danced in the hot July air columns overhead. On the ground chipmunks scampered, and everywhere there were profuse bursts of wildflowers. The scenic beauty of the valley belied the fact that they were following a creature that might be Sasquatch.

"Creatures like Patas Grandes have appeared throughout history," Rosa mused. "In the forest or along a river or lake, whether it's a vampire, a werewolf, the Loch Ness monster, or Grendel."

"I don' know 'bout Grendel," Billy said. "But I met La Llorona once." He laughed.

Rosa laughed with him. "Maybe the more ranchers graze their cattle here, the more they displace the habitat and food of Patas Grandes. It has no choice but to take sheep."

"Sí," Martín said, not sounding as enthusiastic about the hunt as he had in the morning. "Like a wolf sometime come into the valley. Every creature in the world has to eat."

The Mexicanos had long ago settled the valleys that sloped east of the Sacramento Mountains. They raised sheep and cattle, farmed the flatlands along the Bonito and Ruidoso Rivers, where the soil was rich for corn and chile. Apple orchards thrived.

After the Civil War, Texans migrated into the Pecos Valley and the flat eastern llano. Men like John Chisum ran thousands of cattle from Roswell up to Fort Sumner—cattle to feed the U.S. Army and the imprisoned Navajos at Bosque Redondo. In 1864 Kit Carson had destroyed the food crops of the Navajos in Arizona. They had been taken away from their sacred mountains, and they were prisoners of a government that turned a blind eye to their needs. The southerners who migrated into New Mexico didn't have much use for Indians or Mexicans, although a few had married Mexicana women. Cultural prejudices played a role in the ethnic tensions that developed. Mexicanos and Indians were pushed aside as a new wave of migrants began to homestead the fertile cattle country.

Suddenly the horses begin to twitch and pin their ears. Martín pointed. "Always I go north. Lose tracks. Now I know. See the caves. I smell smoke. It cannot be."

Smoke and the aroma of roasting meat, thought Rosa. Did Patas Grandes make a fire to cook the meat?

Martín dismounted and talked calmly to his skittish horse. "Stay with horses," he whispered. "Very nervous, yo voy." The horses had caught a strange scent. Even gentle Mancita was nervous. The scent was strong. Patas Grandes was near.

"I'll go with you," Billy offered.

Martín shook his head. "Mira." He pointed at the sky, which had grown dark and ominous, as if the dark clouds of the mountain spirits protected the creature.

Rosa also looked up into the cloud's dark belly. Were starships watching over Patas Grandes? Marcy's UFO?

Her bracelet tingled. Yes, the starships were near, and it was either Mother Nature or the nature of the universe vibrating with an energy that made her shiver.

But why did Martín insist on going alone? Did he want to meet the creature face to face? It wasn't revenge. Five toes had been around for some time.

"I tell my vecinos to let Patas Grandes take a sheep once in a while," Martín said. "Every animal has to eat. Now I go see."

They watched as Martín made his way toward the dark cave carved into the granite palisade. He paused at the mouth of the cave. A low growl echoed from within. A voice. "Madre mía," Martín said and made the sign of the cross. He was about to come face to face with Patas Grandes, the first man in the valley to do so.

He moved closer until he saw the eyes of Patas Grandes. He aimed his rifle. He had etched a cross on each cartridge. Any evil creature could be killed by the holy power of the cross. He held his aim, heard the low growl, could see the eyes of Patas Grandes. Was the creature speaking? Martín understood a few of the Mescalero words it uttered. At that moment he realized that whatever it was that lived in the cave, it feared men as much as men feared it.

He trembled, felt his arms grow weak, felt his rifle lowering. He stood transfixed, looking at the dark form in the cave. "Soy Martín," he whispered. "Está bien." He turned and made his way back to Billy and Rosa.

"¿Qué pasó?" Billy asked. Martín's face was pale.

"It is not evil," he whispered. "A creature like a man."

Without a further word from Martín, they rode back along the river to Lincoln.

Generations later, the story would be told about Martín and Billy the Kid chasing Patas Grandes up the mountain, but Martín did not kill him. Because, the people said, Patas Grandes was not ChupaCabra, only a creature of the forest, or perhaps of the imagination.

When people heard the story, they smiled and agreed that the ending was as it should be. Patas Grandes was a forest man, not the devil who rode in the whirlwinds of the llano, not a witch who prayed to the devil. He was not to be hunted. He entered the people's imagination and become one more story the elders told children when families gathered to tell stories.

Such creatures could not be killed with bullets. They were part of the storytelling memory of the people. They were the fears that took the form of stories the first humans told ages ago when they lived in caves.

The people said maybe Patas Grandes was a man surviving on the mountain alone. He harmed no one. Let him take a sheep once in a while, Martín had said.

8

Early in the afternoon of April 1, John Middleton burst into Martín and Josefa's house, shouting, "McSween wants us at his place! Sheriff Brady has a warrant on him."

Billy jumped to his feet. "Damn Brady! He let Tunstall's murderers go scot-free." He turned to Rosa. "If you're goin' to write the true history, you might consider this. But it could be dangerous."

"No more dangerous than meeting Saytir. I'm with you."

"¡Vamos!"

They made their way to McSween's, being careful not to be spotted by Brady.

"You know the Anton Chico area?" Billy asked as they walked.

"Yes. An old land grant midway between Las Vegas and Santa Rosa."

"I stopped there once on my way to Las Vegas. The old Hispanos there treated me fine. I played cards in the Las Vegas gambling halls. Beautiful country. Desiderio Romero is sheriff. A good man."

"A good man?"

"Sheriffs like to play cards as much as anyone. Maybe more. Pat Garrett played cards in more saloons than I ever did. He ain't exactly a saint. I played monte with him up in Fort Sumner."

Rosa knew that the trouble between Alexander McSween and James Dolan was about to explode, and Sheriff Brady favored the Dolan and Murphy bunch. Brady and Lawrence Murphy had fought on the Confederate side in the Civil War. They had migrated to Lincoln County early on.

At McSween's, some of Billy's friends had already gathered. The Regulators, they called themselves. They couldn't trust the Lincoln County lawmen, so they considered themselves the law. They were willing to take on Sheriff Brady and serve the warrants they had.

Alexander McSween greeted Rosa graciously. He was a tall,

handsome man. Today he appeared nervous and frightened. He explained his situation. "Sheriff Brady will do anything Dolan orders. They mean to kill me, just as they ordered Tunstall's murder. If Brady serves me with a warrant, I'll be murdered in jail. I'll give a reward to anyone that gets rid of him!"

Billy and the Regulators understood his predicament, and they had no love for the sheriff. Brady had physically abused Charlie Bowdre and George Coe, and he had mistreated Billy and Fred when he was holding them prisoner.

"He took my rifle, an' I aim to get it back," Billy said. "Pistol-whipped me an' Fred for no good reason."

"What do we do?" Middleton asked.

"I aim to get my revenge for Mr. Tunstall's death," Billy said, and the Regulators gathered around him knew what he meant. It was time to get rid of Brady.

"Is there another way?" Rosa asked, then instantly remembered that she was only an observer in a history that had already happened.

"Es mi destino," Billy answered. "This is something I have to do. Otherwise Brady's goin' to treat us like dogs for the rest of our lives."

The men around him nodded in agreement. At one time or another, each of them had felt Brady's wrath.

"Isn't there some other way?" Rosa argued.

Billy smiled. "Don' think so. Ol' man Bonney took good care of me, and he tol' me what you sow you reap. Only a coward wants to take back his life and make it all purty. You best go back to Martín's. There's goin' to be gunfire."

The Arrow of Time, thought Rosa. I can't help him. I'm just here to record what happens. Like any other historian, just take notes.

She grew despondent. It was true, she was caught up in Billy's time because she had made a deal with Marcy, and because of the flash drive. She was along for the ride, but she could do nothing to alter the events of history. Record what she saw on her laptop, and what good would that do? Every writer or storyteller who had ever told what they knew about the life and times of Billy the Kid had made up his own story. Written history wasn't based on immutable facts, it was a telling shaded by all the prejudices, whims, values, and motives of the historian.

Are there no facts in the universe? she asked herself. All the stories, poems, songs, great epics ever written are fiction. Life is a fiction. Life is a dream, as a wise poet said. So you write your own ticket, she thought, as Billy is writing his. But he's just a kid, still a teenager, and I can't help him out of his dilemma. Can we help any child caught up in the revenge his gang has sworn to take?

And so for history to be history, on April 1 Billy Bonney, John Middleton, Henry Brown, Fred Waite, Jim French, and Frank McNab took up positions for an ambush, hiding in the corrals behind the Tunstall store. In a scene straight out of a western movie, Sheriff Brady and four deputies walked the dusty street of Lincoln on their way to the courthouse. On their return, the Regulators opened fire. Rosa watched helplessly from Martín's house as Brady fell dead under a storm of bullets. One of his deputies fell wounded.

Billy leaped over the wall and stood over Brady. "I got my rifle back!" he shouted, waving the weapon. One of the deputies, Billy Mathews, watching from the Cisneros home, shot at Billy and hit him in the thigh. Rosa gasped as Billy hobbled back to the corral wall. Minutes later, he stumbled into Martín's.

Josefa rushed to help him to a chair. "Sit here," she said, taking charge. You got a bullet, Bilito!"

"It's nothin'. Just punched my thigh. But we got to get out of Lincoln. The law-abidin' citizens are goin' to want my blood."

Billy gulped down the pitcher of water Josefa served him while she cleaned the superficial wound and bound it with a strip of cloth she had cut from a sheet. "Feel better," she said.

"Gracias, Josefa. Eres mi madrecita." Billy hugged her. It was true; he had no other mother.

"Anda," Josefa said, blushing. "You are big baby. In this territory a woman learns to deliver babies and clean gunshot wounds. Bury the dead."

Martín had gone out in the street with the other vecinos. "Brady's dead," he said on returning. "Took eight bullets."

Rosa bowed her head. Billy said nothing at first, whistling a tune as he wiped the barrel of his Winchester '73 carbine, a repeater that held twelve .44-.40 centerfire cartridges. Billy was never separated from the Winchester, and Rosa guessed he even slept with it. And with his pistol, a Colt double-action .41-caliber.

After a few moments, he looked up and spoke. "It's war," he said. "There be no murder when you're at war. They killed Tunstall, now we're even."

"It is true," Josefa said, comforting Rosa. "The Dolans make war on Mr. Tunstall. Dolan controls all things. Many vecinos lose their ranchos."

"We must protect ourself," Martín added.

"Code of the West," Rosa said.

"Code of war," Billy replied. "This is war, an' you can call it the Lincoln County War. A man can kill for a cause. Besides, not just my bullet kilt him. All of us fired"

"But they blame you," Josefa said. "Best you hide."

"Yeah. We're headed for Tularosa. Hide out for a while. Rosa can stay."

"Yes, we take care of her. Ay, Dios, what bad time come to our valley. Do not blame Bilito, Rosa. There is no law here. We protect our familias, our casas."

"I'll be back in a couple of days. Got to finish the mission," Billy said.

"You sure you can ride?" Rosa asked.

"I'm fine. You stay here. Adiós." He went out limping, laughing, calling, "No man born yet who can kill Billy Bonney!"

"A terrible day," Josefa said. "I worry. You worry too," she said to Rosa.

"Yes."

"You know what will happen," she intoned softly. She went to the bucket of water at the trastero, spooned out a cupful, and made Rosa drink. "You rest." She led a shaken Rosa to the large pantry, which held a cot and quilts. "Rest," she said. "We love Bilito like a son. We do not like the killing, but here life is cheap. Every vaquero has a gun, and all protect himself. Ay, Dios, que triste."

Rosa lay down but could not sleep. The hot day wore slowly into twilight as the town of Lincoln dealt with the day's event. Many were filled with outrage and indignation at the murder of the sheriff. Whatever sympathy the town had had for McSween evaporated. Rosa had already written the chapter in her novel about the shootout with Sheriff Brady, but writing was distanced from the real event. Being there, hearing the barrage of gunfire, smelling the gunsmoke, seeing the sheriff fall dead . . . that was real. How much truth did she want? She knew there had been bad feelings between the sheriff and Billy's gang, the Regulators. The rifle the sheriff carried belonged to Billy, and Billy was determined to get it back.

When the shooting had stopped and Billy rushed to take the rifle from the dead sheriff, he was shaking, his face flushed. His voice was trembling. He tried to hide his emotions, but he couldn't. It was a Billy Rosa hadn't seen before. The truth was that Billy the Kid was not a cold-blooded killer. Rosa had wanted to reach out and comfort him, but she couldn't touch him. She was from a distant time, and she, too, was still shaking from the tragic event.

Rosa got up off the cot and sat down with her laptop. In the chaos of the day, she had not set up her solar charger, and she worried that the battery would soon run low. She looked up at the well-thumbed calendar on the wall: 1878.

"Marcy," she typed, "I don't understand how time is working. How long will I be here?"

"As long as it takes to get the true story. That's what you want, isn't it?"

"Yes, I know, it's what every writer wants, but do I have to witness every event? The killing of the sheriff was horrible. The gunfight was something I never thought I'd experience. I felt I was in hell."

"Sometimes you have to go to hell to get the truth," Marcy answered. "You want to go back on your deal?"

Rosa answered no.

She was going to be present as Billy's life unraveled, right up to the destined day, July 14, 1881, in Fort Sumner. She thought of her friend CiCi working on her own Bilito book, safe behind her desk. I wish I could call home, Rosa thought. There's no phone. Of course there's no phone! No electricity. No running water. No refrigerators. No blenders. They kill a pig, and the meat is shared with vecinos the same day. No way to keep it cold. Kill a steer, and what you don't share with neighbors you use to make carne seca. Jerky. Thin slices of meat hanging on the clothesline to dry in the sun.

She listlessly emailed her father. "Wish I was home . . ."

Moments later, a reply shone on her screen. "Rosa, so pleased to hear from you. How are you? Are you in Puerto de Luna? How's the book coming? Love, Dad."

Rosa's lips trembled; she felt her hands go numb. She was in Lincoln, in 1878. Time was reversed, as she had come to accept, but her email had reached her father in Santa Fe. Sitting at his desk, probably reading a newspaper on his computer, he had opened her message. How?

Were the metaphysical waves of the universe not subject to the Arrow of Time? Was the world going on about its normal business, and only she was caught in a parallel universe?

"I am fine . . . ," she typed when her fingers grew steady.

9

When Rosa awoke, she was briefly startled by the surroundings. She was lying on a cot in Josefa's large pantry. Her eyes took in the jars of preserves and jellies sitting on the shelves, muslin sacks full of dehydrated apple slices and green chile, carne seca hanging from the ceiling, bins full of sugar, flour, pinto beans, and lard. With no refrigerators, everything had to be dehydrated. She remembered the luscious apple pies her mother had made from dried apple slices.

She had seen Sheriff Brady gunned down and had hoped that maybe sleep would erase the fright she felt. Weren't dreams another way to escape ordinary reality? Dreams came from a time and place no one could control. In dreams, the dreamer could wander in and out of events and times that couldn't be imagined in real time. If there was such a thing as real time.

She wasn't in real time, she was in Billy's time, April 1, 1878, Lincoln County, New Mexico. How could she dream in a time that was not real to her? Would dreams only take her deeper into . . . what?

Rosa pinched herself and felt it. "This is no joke," she whispered. She got up and walked into the kitchen. Josefa had left a plate with food on the table. Rosa lifted the towel, exposing beans, fried potatoes, a slice of meat, and Josefa's canned peaches for dessert. The large blue enameled coffee pot on the stove was still warm.

Rosa silently thanked Josefa, but she wasn't hungry. Something told her that her adventure with Billy had to end. She had stepped into his life, but now it was time to get out. From what she had read, the life of Billy the Kid would only get more violent as it wound down to his fateful day in Fort Sumner, New Mexico.

What was she supposed to do, ride with him? Become a member of the gang? No, Billy's life, then and now, was his. It was his destino, as he said. *His* destiny, she thought to herself. I have mine.

In the bedroom beyond the kitchen, she heard snoring. Martín and Josefa were asleep. The sheriff had been killed, but they had to go on with their lives. For the struggling Mexicano farmers of Lincoln County, the war raged on. The violent times attracted outlaws to the area, and the poor and honest people were caught in the middle.

Rosa took out her laptop and wrote: "Only five years earlier, the Horrell clan, who hated the Mexicano natives, had attacked Lincoln and killed Juan Patrón's father and three other men. Bloodshed was not new to Lincoln County.

"Citizens from Lincoln north to Las Vegas were caught up in the same violence that affected the country after the Civil War. The migration from east to west, which Turner described as building the American democracy, was paid for dearly by native populations.

"My mother's ancestors had settled in Puerto de Luna, once the county seat of Guadalupe County before it was moved to Santa Rosa. My grandparents had lived through the tremendous changes that came with the Anglo, los Americanos as the people called them.

"The old-timers still told stories of Billy the Kid's sojourns into Puerto de Luna. He didn't drink, he loved to dance, and he romanced some of the young girls—that is, if they could escape from the watchful eyes of their parents in that traditional culture."

Ah, so much history, Rosa sighed, closing the laptop and slipping out the front door into the night. In the corral Mancita snorted, aware of Rosa. In the hills a coyote called, then all was quiet. No dogs barked. The town was asleep.

The weak moon cast a pale bluish light over the landscape. It was just enough light for Rosa to walk down to the river. She was near the stream when a growl in the thick brush made her freeze. She held her breath. Maybe it was just a coyote, or a black bear scavenging in the village dump. Her worst fear was realized when she turned and saw two fierce reptilian eyes staring at her. It was one of Saytir's Himits!

Stupid, she said to herself. Look what you've gotten into. She picked up a stick and stepped back.

"Won't do you much good," the Himit said.

Rosa knew the clones could change form, but this one was fearful beyond description: eyes burning with liquid fire, dark greenish scales covering its body, ugly claws instead of hands. If the Himit had come to instill fear, it succeeded. Rosa felt her energy drain, and a cold sweat made her shiver.

"Shouting won't do much good either," it growled. "Your friend Billy is dancing in Tularosa."

Rosa took another step backward. She knew she couldn't outrun a Himit. Not in the dark.

"Saytir sends his regards. You fooled him on the bridge, and loving the games as he does, he gives you credit. But this game's over. Saytir sent me to settle a score. You killed one of ours in Roswell. You have the flash drive. Hand it over."

"I buried it," Rosa said.

"It belongs to C-Force!" the Himit shouted. "We want it!"

"You'll use it to make war," Rosa replied.

"Don't blame your war games on us! You humans have been making war since long before our scientists created us. We will make you humans our slaves. Science has created a superior life form, part ChupaCabra DNA, part space alien. The aliens' intelligence is far superior to humans'. In fact, Saytir thinks humans have very little intelligence. That's why your different nations keep destroying each other."

The Himit laughed.

"Go to hell!" Rosa shouted. "You're monsters! Automatons! You can't think for yourselves! When you die, you turn to slime! You have no heart! No feelings!" Her anger came rushing out, and with that outburst she was sure that she had sealed her fate. The Himit did not like to be called the Cyborg of a new age.

"Then die!" it cried and struck, a blow that sent Rosa reeling to the ground. "Die! And your friends, too, will die!"

Before it could strike again, a large, burly figure came crashing out of the brush, striking at the Himit with a huge club. "Billy!" Rosa cried. But it wasn't Billy. The figure was covered with hair like a gorilla. His cry was bloodthirsty, and the blows he struck at the Himit were powerful and deadly. The Himit fought back, striking and clawing at the formidable opponent it had not expected. The fury of the gorilla-man was too much for the Himit. The battle was quickly over. The gorilla-man cracked the Himit's skull, and it fell to the earth and melted into slimy liquid.

The struggle done, the gorilla-man turned to Rosa. Panting, he stood over her, then took her hand and helped her to her feet. He uttered a low growl, as if wishing to communicate. Although Rosa was in shock, she understood that the gorilla-man meant her no harm. Was this a humanoid, something evolved from convergent evolution? Parallel evolution? Evolved from dinosaurs like birds?

The growl came again. Words formed, or seemed to form, and Rosa heard something like "Go home." Did he mean for Rosa to go home? Again the low utterance escaped softly from his mouth. "Go home."

"Go home?" Rosa replied. The gorilla-man nodded, then turned and disappeared in the river brush, leaving a confused Rosa wondering what the message meant. Did he mean she was supposed to go home? Was there more danger ahead for her? She didn't know how to go home. She was trapped in Billy's time, and she had to see the unfolding story to the end.

Rosa's thoughts swirled in a new direction. "Wait a minute," she whispered. What if it was the creature who wanted to go home? His home was not in the Sierra Blanca, his home was somewhere else. But where? Suddenly it hit her. Patas Grandes is Sasquatch! His home is the Pacific Northwest, not here! He wants to return home. But how? And how did he get here? A tribe from the cold Northwest had come to visit the Mescaleros. Did the ceremony they performed transport him here? Did the Mescaleros have to take him home? Could sacred ceremonies be that powerful?

Is this why Martín wouldn't kill Sasquatch? He understood that the creature was a humanoid. Martín was close to the Mescaleros. He attended their dances and ceremonies. Some of the first Mexicanos who had come to settle in the valleys at the foot of the Sierra Blanca had married Mescalero women. A ceremony! Of course! But could ceremonies be that strong? Rosa believed that communal ceremonies and dances created sacred space. The Kachina and Matachine dances of the New Mexico pueblos created sacred space. Rosa had been there, she had experienced the dances as an act of faith, like being in church. For thousands of years the native people had danced, and their communities had prospered.

For Rosa the Catholic mass created sacred space. God the Great Spirit came down during the mass. Did those sacred ceremonies create an opening in space-time? Did they create wormholes?

"That's it!" Rosa cried. Martín would speak to the Mescaleros. Explain that Sasquatch had to get back to his home in the Pacific Northwest. They would hold dances, a ceremony that would transport Sasquatch back home. "What am I thinking?" she said to herself. "It's ridiculous!" She turned and hurried up the path to the safety of Josefa's home.

10

Rosa wrote furiously. Whatever was happening in Lincoln County was a microcosm of what was happening in the western territories. After the Civil War, Americans had poured west, families seeking a new home and land to farm, but also men seeking adventure, a new life, and wealth. Native Americans were not only pushed out of their native lands, they suffered a genocide. The so-called Code of the West evolved as reckless men seeking power pushed aside or killed whoever stood in their path. The Code of the West was born in the East.

In Lincoln County, the McSween and Dolan/Murphy factions interpreted the Code of the West as a justification for war, and killing in time of war was dismissed as just cause. Both sides did what they had to do to win advantage.

Empire building had its destructive side. The West was the new battleground, from Washington, D.C., to the goldfields of California, where the forty-niners ran rampant over the native populations. A killing fever spread west. The country was moving west, where there was space and new fortunes to be made. Crooked politicians allowed nothing to stand in their way. Manifest Destiny encouraged men to grab what they could.

Yes, the Lincoln County War reflected the times.

But the murder of Sheriff Brady and the killing of William McCloskey, Frank Baker, and Billy Morton went beyond the limits of a lax ethical code. Good men began to take notice and condemn the outlaw gangs.

Rosa wrote Marcy: "A Himit attacked me last night. Red eyes, claws . . . I was saved by . . . never mind, that is a long, complicated story."

Marcy wrote back: "Rosa, be careful. I think C-Force used a super 3D printer to construct the Himits. They farmed alien DNA and injected it into ChupaCabras. What else? Apparently some Himits like Saytir are super-morphing beasts. Transformers in monster bodies. C-Force wants the flash drive because all the formulas they used are on it. They lost the original formulas and all the biomedical engineering data when Nadine drove her car into their labs, including what they had stored in the cloud. The flash drive is it. The president wants it, and he'll do anything to get it. I don't know what to tell you . . . be careful . . . stay with Billy."

Cybernetic organisms created by science gone mad. Maybe C-Force couldn't be stopped. If they had the flash drive, C-Force at the bidding of the president could create Himits beyond belief. Was humanity doomed?

What should I do? Billy said to bury it. Where? Why? Saytir followed us through the wormhole. If I go back with the flash drive, he'll follow me. What if C-Force is testing Saytir? No flash drive and they kill him to get components for a new Cyborg. How long does Saytir's power last? The questions spun in Rosa's brain. The only thing she could do was write her notes.

The life of Billy and his gang of vaqueros was not as romantic as the western movies portrayed it. When in town among friends they attended the bailes, where Billy excelled at the foot-stomping polkas, the waltzes, and square dancing, and his favorite, "Turkey in the Straw." He was an expert at card games, especially monte.

When the gang was on the run from the law, they had to hide out in sheep camps, where the Mexicanos always made Billy feel welcome. Or bunk with friends at ranches, where accommodations were raw and primitive. Winter blizzards swept across the Llano Estacado, making travel nearly impossible.

Summers were also torturous. Riding a horse for ten or fifteen miles when the temperature often rose over a hundred was killing on man and beast. Mirages floated across the open plain east of Pecos. Whirlwinds rose like cyclones. When rain came, it battered the earth and turned thirsty dust into treacherous mud.

There were three seasons on the Llano Estacado: freezing cold, burning hot—and wind.

Where once the buffalo roamed, now huge herds of Chisum and Goodnight cattle fed on rich prairie grass. Where once the Kiowa and the Comanches were lords of the land, now thousands of sheep grazed. Sheep camps and ranches dotted the vast plain. There were fortunes to be made in providing cattle, sheep, and horses to the U.S. Army.

Cattle rustling was common. Many a vaquero was known to run into a herd on the range and stop to cut aside a few steers. After the brand was altered, the cattle could be quickly sold. Billy and his friends were no different. When they came across a herd of horses, they would drive off a few and sell them to ranchers who would buy and not look at the brand.

Rustling kept the gang in money for provisions. Most ranchers turned a blind eye to a little rustling, but soon the big ranchers began to unite to protect their interests.

These thoughts were on Rosa's mind as she rode with Billy toward Blazer's Mills on April 4. Billy had returned with the Regulators, and Lincoln was loath to welcome him.

"Ride with me," he told Rosa. "You will see for yourself the real story. Let time bring what it will."

Rosa knew what it would bring. She knew the history. Billy's fate was written in the stars, and he could not alter their movement. Was predestination wrapped into the Arrow of Time? No one could escape. That's what Rosa felt.

"Saytir's still around," he said, flashing his disarming smile. "You come with me, and you will not only write *The True Story of Billy Bonney*, you will also find the right place to bury the flash drive."

Following him held no rhyme nor reason, because reason operated in real time, where clocks ticked off the hours, not in the wormhole that held her captive. She had to follow her instincts, and those emotions felt timeless. What did she have left? Only her survival instinct.

Or was it a romantic invitation? Rosa shook her head. No, she didn't think of Billy in a romantic way. True, he had a style young women admired. He was young, cheerful, a great dancer, always jovial. Josefa said he had plenty of queridas, from Lincoln to Puerto de Luna.

Rosa followed him because she had made up her mind to write his true story. Had she sold her soul to the devil? Could she throw away all her notes, be done with the life-threatening compulsion to write the true story, and wake up to a normal day in her house in Puerto de Luna?

"Vamos," she said, deciding to ride with the fourteen Regulators to Blazer's Mills near the Mescalero Indian Agency.

She enjoyed the ride through the mountains and down into the Río Tularosa. Whatever premonitions she had about violence, she had to swallow. She knew the history, but to live it she had to put it out of her mind. Pretend she didn't know. She couldn't sway Billy to change his ways. The die was cast. What happened could not be changed.

That day the opposing forces met at the mill. The Regulators thought Buckshot Roberts had been with Billy Morton when his posse killed Tunstall, and they had a warrant for his arrest. By coincidence, that day Buckshot rode into Blazer's Mills to pick up his mail. The Regulators, camped in the corral, spotted him.

"¿Quién es?" Billy asked.

"It's Buckshot," Frank Coe answered.

"We got him dead."

"Let me talk to him. See if he will surrender." Rosa watched as Coe tried to talk Buckshot into giving up.

"I give up and the Kid will kill me," Buckshot argued loudly. Time passed, and the Regulators grew impatient.

Suddenly Charlie Bowdre rushed Buckshot, shouting for him to surrender. Both fired at the same time, and Buckshot took a bullet in the stomach. Buckshot's bullet hit John Middleton in the chest. Blood pouring from his stomach, Buckshot limped toward Rosa and pointed his pistol at her. "You're next!" he shouted. Just then Dick Brewer rushed him. Buckshot took aim and fired, and Brewer took a bullet that blew away half of his skull.

Rosa ran to Billy, who grabbed her and pushed her to the ground. "Keep down! Buckshot just killed Brewer!"

The air was acrid with gunsmoke and dust raised by the nervous horses, the sweat of the men, adrenaline making itself known in the cursing and shouting, the nauseating smell of violence, and Rosa was caught in it. She covered her ears, sank into the straw-covered ground, and waited. After a while, the shooting stopped; the men did not want to go in after Buckshot.

I am not the cause nor the end of this history, Rosa said to herself. Please, dear Virgin, grant I may return home safely.

Brewer was dead, and Buckshot lay mortally wounded. And for what? That is the question she would have to answer if she was to make sense of the terrible tragedies she was witness to. It was the same question she had wrestled with when she counseled barrio kids in LA. Why did they form gangs, and why were they willing to die for the gang? What was the bond that held the gang together?

Survival. Since primitive times, men have bonded together to keep the clan alive. War creates brotherhoods of men. Semper fi. Airborne. Seals. Green Berets. City kids with little hope found family and acceptance in the gang and their labels: homeboys, tattoos, la vida loca, skinheads, labels of bonding, hundreds of labels.

It was no different in Lincoln County. Rosa realized that often the individual gang members didn't understand the overarching powers that controlled most of their behavior. Both McSween and Dolan were intent on building empires, but they paid the vaqueros meager wages, so the wealth at the top did not trickle down to the gang members. Didn't they understand this?

Once the Regulators bonded, the stamp of loyalty became the members' prime motive. The bigger picture didn't matter. They lost sight of the fact that the powerful forces that had started the war in the first place cared little for them. Rosa had seen this occur in the drug wars of LA, and it was true in every city in the country. The little guys fought and killed each other; the big guys made the money.

"It's over," Billy said, interrupting her thoughts. "I know what you're thinking, but Buckshot was there when they killed Tunstall. So he paid."

11

Things were moving too fast for Rosa to write complete notes on the events. She thought perhaps the recording of history had pretty much always been like this; from prehistoric paintings on cave walls to Homer's poetry, stories from those who had lived in the past. Herodotus wrote accounts of the Persian Wars, which he called historiai, in which he included observations about everything of interest to him.

Did that mean anything of interest could be called history? Where lay the actual facts on which history rested? Was the oral tradition history? Were stories history? Walt Whitman's poems were history. Denise Chávez's latest novel was history. All poetry was history.

She fished out her laptop and wrote Marcy. "Everyone is caught up in history. Maybe history is nothing more than a measure of the propagation of the species. One generation leads to the next."

"Could be," was Marcy's response.

"Damn it! You're not being helpful." She closed the laptop.

In 1848, U.S. imperialism took all of Mexico's northern territories in an unjust war. It seemed as if half the country headed west, families in covered wagons hoping for a better future. Down the Santa Fe Trail they came, stopping at Bent's Fort, where they looked toward the New Mexico Territory as their new home.

Josefa had given Rosa a saddlebag for her laptop, along with a pair of leather pants, chaps, wool shirts, a vest, and one of Martín's old sombreros. She stored the clothes in her backpack. She realized that her life was on hold. All those responsibilities waiting for her in her own time would have to wait. For the moment she felt free of responsibility, and therein lay the allure of riding with the vaqueros.

She had enjoyed the ride to Blazer's Mills with the Regulators, Billy's vaqueros. Riding Mancita gave her a sense of freedom, the wind in her face, the beauty of the landscape. Often, Billy sang. He knew verses from many songs, and riding at a slow pace listening to him sing added to the peacefulness of the landscape.

> Yo soy el muchacho alegre
> que me divierto cantando,
> Las madres que tengan hijas
> tenganse mucho cuidado,
> yo soy el muchacho alegre,
> y soy muy enamorado.*

Sometimes there was sadness in his song:

> No tengo padre ni madre
> ni quien se duela de mí.
> Solo la cama en que duermo
> se compadece de mí.†

The songs came from the repertoire of New Mexico folk music, and when Rosa heard him sing, it opened up another view into his soul.

She did not condone the killings, but she was not responsible for what happened and could not stop it. So why not enjoy the moment, a time that would never come again. No wonder the young were so reckless: in their undeveloped brains, they realized that youth could never be lived again. So carpe diem!

They were having coffee when Billy and the vaqueros arrived: Coe, Middleton, Brown, Waite, and Bowdre. A loosely knit band of

---

*I am a happy young fellow
Who finds contentment in singing,
Let the mothers with daughters
Watch over them very carefully,
For I'm a happy young fellow,
Full of love's sweet emotion.

†I have neither father nor mother
no one who cares for me.
Only the bed where I sleep
takes pity on me.

vaqueros she was beginning to know, men who accepted her ethereal presence because of Billy. They knew the bond between her and the Kid was not a romantic thing. It had to do with the small black box she carried, but they said nothing. She was writing the Kid's story, he was protecting her, and that was it.

"District Attorney Rynerson is a sumbitch," Billy drawled. "He sides with Dolan. Indicted me for the murder of Sheriff Brady, an' he has a warrant for Charlie Bowdre for killing Buckshot."

"We have warrants on Dolan's buzzards," Coe said. "We are a lawful posse. They cain't just heap the blame on you."

Rosa knew that George Coe was one of Billy's closest allies.

"Tom Catron took Dolan's store," Martín said. "Confiscado. The store está cerrado."

"And a new sheriff," Josefa added. "Copeland."

"He's got a warrant for us," Bowdre said. "And we got warrants for them. Let's see who serves them first."

"Forgot about Rynerson an' warrants," Billy said, smiling. "Let's party. Mary is playing her piano at McSween's. I feel like singin' an' stompin'." There was nothing Billy enjoyed more than singing around a piano.

"I bring my violin," Martín offered.

"I'll need to take a bath," Rosa said, looking at Josefa. Josefa looked at Martín and the vaqueros. They looked puzzled.

"River's too cold," Billy said.

Cowboys only took an occasional bath in the summer when the water wasn't freezing. "Not even the ricos take bath," Martín said. "Mucho frío."

"I cain't remember my last bath," John Middleton intoned. The vaqueros laughed uneasily.

"Me either," Bowdre said.

"But Rosa is a lady," Josefa said. "Martín, get the cajete. Get me water. We fix a bath."

The cowboys shrugged. Women were different. They needed baths. Taking baths was a newfangled idea.

One by one the vaqueros drifted out, shaking their heads. When Billy walked by, he winked. "Roses don' need baths. They always smell sweet."

"If it's not too much trouble," Rosa protested.

"No, no trouble," Josefa insisted. "A young lady needs a bath to go to dance. This is special."

Martín brought in the large washtub, placed it in front of the huge wood-burning stove, then returned with buckets of water. Josefa threw piñon logs into the stove and heated the water. "Here all the vaqueros smell," she said when Rosa was settled in the sudsy water. "They take no baths. For why? They all smell the same." She laughed, and Rosa laughed with her. She liked the stout, energetic woman, and she vowed to forgo the luxury of the next bath until she could bathe in the river.

When the bath was done, Josefa brought out a plain blue taffeta dress. "My marriage," she said. "Was young, not so fat." She laughed. "Time changes everything." The dress fit Rosa. "You are like a daughter. All the vaqueros want to dance with you." She offered Rosa a piece of oshá. "A root," she said. "You chew and make the breath sweet. Billy chew oshá, and that is why the muchachas like to dance with him."

That evening, Billy and the vaqueros picked up Rosa. They looked like slick cats after a good grooming. Martín had given away their secret. "The river is freezing in April, pero they all jump in and take a bath. The vecinos thought they were drunk, but no. Maybe they don' want smell too bad." He laughed, and Rosa and Josefa had to laugh with him.

Billy took Rosa's hand and walked her down the street to the McSween home, the vaqueros trailing. The village Hispanos came out to see the parade. Everyone cheered, for they loved Billy and thought Rosa was his novia, and any moment of gaiety was welcomed in the troubled times.

Mary played Sue McSween's piano, and Martín played his fiddle. Billy danced every polka and waltz. Some of the local young women had come to the party. Each stood by waiting for Billy to ask her to dance, and each wondered why Billy danced more often with Rosa.

"Turkey in the Straw," he shouted, and those who knew the song joined him in singing.

Turkey in the hay, in the hay, in the hay.
Turkey in the straw, in the straw, in the straw.
Pick up your fiddle and rosin your bow,
And put on a tune called Turkey in the Straw.

They sang and danced late into the night, but no one could keep pace with Billy. Accompanied by Martín, he sang a variety of folk songs. He loved singing and knew many ballads. That night he seemed the happiest of young men.

The party ended with Mary's parting song:

O you'll take the high road, and I'll take the low road,
And I'll be in Scotland before you,
But me and my true love will never meet again,
On the bonnie, bonnie banks of Loch Lomond.

On the way home, a thoughtful Rosa sang softly, "O you'll take the high road, and I'll take the low road, and I'll be in Puerto de Luna before you . . ." When will I ever be home, she wondered.

Something about the Kid was prophetic. The next day, April 30, when most of the rancheros were out burning winter brush in their fields and caring for their flocks, a Dolan posse rode into Lincoln to arrest the Regulators. Rosa watched as the sides took up firing positions and exchanged gunfire. George Coe shot and killed "Dutch Charlie" Kruling, an innocent man who got caught in the crossfire. He turned out to be the only casualty of that battle. A bullet hit Juan Patrón's front door during the gunfight, but he was not hurt.

The more adventurous village boys climbed up on rooftops to watch the gunplay. Not a good idea, since that's how Kruling was killed. Rosa knew these boys were accustomed to gunfire. They admired Billy and imitated his horsemanship, practicing riding at a full gallop and shooting at targets. What would become of them? she wondered. Will they become farmers and ranchers like their fathers, or choose the wild life of vaqueros?

These were the same boys whose fathers had only twenty years earlier taken potshots at the retreating Confederate Army of General Sibley. The Texans had to retreat after they lost the Battle of Glorieta Pass east of Santa Fe. That spring of 1861, the Mexicano population and Apaches, who had no love for the Texans, made the retreat as miserable as possible.

Four hours later, the gun battle between Dolan and the Regulators was still blazing when Lieutenant Smith arrived from Fort Stanton with twenty black cavalrymen, the famed Buffalo Soldiers who had taken part in the Indian Wars. Smith stopped the gunfight and conducted the Dolan posse back to Fort Stanton. The battle was over. The boys on the rooftops cheered. The relieved Mexicano farmers and ranchers returned to their spring work. Even in the turbulent times there was work to be done, shearing sheep, fixing the young bulls, providing for home and family.

The following day, Billy returned to Martín's home for Rosa. "How'd you like the party?"

"No wonder the señoritas love to dance with you," Rosa responded.

"My sweet mother taught me," Billy said. "An' you dance like an angel."

Rosa blushed. What would her niece Belinda say? She had felt a thrill when she floated across the dance floor in Billy's arms. Did he feel romance when he looked into her eyes? Had she felt romance? Maybe a deep friendship. She had to keep reminding herself that she could not change the Arrow of Time that was taking Billy to his appointed date with fate.

"Ready to ride?"

"Another gunfight?" she asked.

"No, Dolan's back at Fort Stanton. We're goin' to Seven Rivers. Got a warrant to arrest un hombre muy malo." He laughed.

Yes, she was ready. Josefa had told her to keep the blue taffeta dress, which she stuffed in her backpack. A reminder of the party, a reminder of her femininity. She thanked Josefa and Martín for their hospitality.

"You come back with Bilito," Josefa said. "Esta es tu casa."

Rosa hugged her. "Gracias. I will come back."

Could she be sure of her return? What if there were an accident and she died in time past? Was that possible?

12

Led by Doc Scurlock, the Regulators, including several Mexicanos, rode to Seven Rivers. There they met up with Josefita Chávez, an appointed deputy in the Regulators' posse. She was also the leader of the Mexicanos. Rosa had not previously met Josefita, but she had heard that the woman had no fear. She rode with the Regulators because she felt the Dolan gang was subjugating her people. For her, Dolan was far worse than McSween.

When they camped at night, Rosa sought out Josefita, but her stare told Rosa she didn't have time. "Maybe soon," she said as she hustled around the camp, ordering the cook to start the potatoes and meat, warm the tortillas they had packed, and brew a large pot of coffee. She ordered two Mexicanos to guard the perimeter of the camp. After supper she said goodnight to Rosa, curled up in her serape, and slept.

Josefita reminded Rosa of the Adelitas, the Mexican women who in another forty years would fight alongside their men during the Mexican Revolution. The revolution would give rise to men like Zapata and Pancho Villa, men whose names would become part of history. The Mexican legacy would also enshrine the Adelitas in song and in the memory of the people. But all that still awaited in the future.

It was obvious that Billy and the vaqueros respected her, but there was little communication between them. She and the Mexicanos were riding to safeguard their own interests: to preserve the land that was being encroached on by the Americanos. They would give their lives to protect their traditional way of life. Rosa knew that both Dolan and McSween had tried to get the Mexicanos involved in the war. They hoped to split the Hispano community, pitting one side against the other. If such a fight ensued, Hispanos from as far north as Taos might be drawn into the struggle. It's been done in all wars, Rosa thought, persuading the local natives to fight on your side. Cortés conquered Mexico by using Indian allies who hated the Aztecs. The U.S. had done the same in its war against Native Americans. War and suffering seemed to become entwined in the Arrow of Time, and the history of most nations was often taught as a history of wars fought.

On May 15, the Regulators reached Seven Rivers, seized some horses, and proceeded to stampede the Dolan herd. They took the cook prisoner, a man named Manuel Segovia, also known as el Indio. The Regulators had a warrant for him, accusing him of killing a fellow Regulator, Frank McNab. Billy and the others were thirsty for revenge. Amid the lathered horses and the dust raised by the scattering herd, Segovia begged for mercy.

"Sumbitch rode with the Mathews posse," Bowdre cursed. "They bushwhacked McNab, Coe, and Saunders."

"He killed McNab," Scurlock said. "Our warrant's good."

Realizing he was a dead man, Segovia, quick as a cougar, suddenly swung up on Bowdre's horse, grabbed his pistol, and pushed him to the ground. "Get him, Billy!" Scurlock shouted. Josefita and Billy spurred their horses and took up the chase. They rode into the dust of the stampede and into a small arroyo, all the while exchanging gunfire with Segovia.

"I hope he gets his." An embarrassed Bowdre cursed and dusted himself off. After a few minutes, all was quiet. Rosa held her breath and waited. They all waited until Josefita and Billy emerged from the arroyo.

"Warrant served," Billy said.

"He got what he deserved," Josefita added, handing an embarrassed Bowdre his horse's reins. "Next time be careful with mountain lion."

Segovia had paid his dues. The Regulators rode back to Lincoln.

Thomas B. Catron was the most powerful politician in the territory. He complained vigorously to Governor Axtell in Santa Fe about the Brady killing. At the same time, the U.S. Interior and Justice Department began looking into the killing of Tunstall. The British foreign office had complained about the murder of a British subject. Depositions were being taken, in which Billy and friends told their accounts of the fight.

During this time, Josefa and Rosa were invited to tea by the local schoolteacher. María Facio's family had migrated from Mexico, and she had been educated at an academy in Santa Fe. "I teach my Mexican children," she told Rosa. "Santa Fe provides little resources. We have many children, but since New Mexico became a territory, we seem to be forgotten. The people here help pay my salary, and we have a one-room schoolhouse. It is a struggle."

María knew firsthand how difficult it was to get an education. Two years at the academy had qualified her as a teacher. She realized the time of the gringo had come to New Mexico, and the Mexicano kids needed an education, especially in English.

"I am single," she said. "Some of the young men of the town say I am strange. Living alone, not married."

"They are tontos," Josefa scoffed. "A beautiful young girl like you. You have education. All they know is cows."

María sighed. "I choose to teach. We need teachers. There is so much to do. So I am happy." She showed Rosa her bookcase, a rarity for the time. "Every penny I save goes to buy books."

Rosa looked at the books, mostly grammars and readers, a few novels, Jane Austen, Melville, Hawthorne, a copy of the Treaty of Guadalupe Hidalgo, Whitman's *Leaves of Grass* from 1855, and Mark Twain's 1873 novel *The Gilded Age: A Tale of Today*. "I read this when I was in college," she mused, picking up the book.

"Where were you educated?" María asked.

Rosa stammered. "I mean, I thought I had read it." Here was her dilemma again. How could she explain that she had been educated at the University of New Mexico when in this time it didn't even exist yet?

"You are welcome to borrow it. It just arrived from Santa Fe. What is going on here is a reflection of what's happening on the East Coast. The rich bankers have taken over the country. In Santa Fe the corrupt politicians and their cronies have taken over our territory. Wall Street robber barons, they're called. Here they are cattle barons."

"And land barons," Josefa said. "Greed make men crazy. We settle this land, have cows, garden, our church, school for los niños. Now greed make the war."

"Yes," Rosa agreed. The two women understood the change coming to the land. The Arrow of Time was marching relentlessly forward, creating a class of rich industrialists in the East. Their unethical values were spreading across the country. Factories on the East Coast needed the immigrants arriving at Ellis Island. Cheap labor made the rich richer and left the working poor struggling to feed their families.

"The Gilded Age in the New Mexico Territory," Rosa said, holding the book. "I never thought of it that way."

"Yes," María replied. "Dolan and McSween are men who want to get rich. The railroad has reached Alburquerque. In a few years it will be in El Paso. The Homestead Act passed fifteen years ago has brought many Americanos to this country. They all want land."

"And water," Josefa added. "Our rivers."

"We are living in a time of great change," María said. "That is why we must educate our children. Teach them to take care of themselves. The politicians in Santa Fe do little for us."

"Maybe Billy can help," Rosa said, her voice rising.

María smiled. "Bilito has a kind heart, that is why the people love him. But he is accused of murder. Billy is caught in a time he does not fully understand. Twain's book tells us that greed creates a time of violence. Those at the top care little for those at the bottom."

Yes, thought Rosa, Billy knows that the Mexicanos are losing their land and irrigation water. That is why he's on their side. Meeting María and Josefa had given her a broader understanding of the time, but with each new revelation she grew despondent. There was nothing she could do to change the coming events. She could not save Billy.

13

This has the makings of a Greek tragedy, thought Rosa as she made her way down the dusty main street of Lincoln.

Billy is Achilles out to avenge the death of Tunstall. The wrath of Achilles was set loose when his best friend, Patroclus, was killed. Achilles of the fearful sword, Billy of the fast gun.

Patroclus went into battle wearing Achilles' armor, and the Trojans, thinking it was Achilles, attacked him with a vengeance. When he heard the news of his friend's death, Achilles blamed himself.

Billy feels that he got there too late to save Tunstall.

Achilles was destined to die at Troy, the fates had decreed it, and since no man knows his fate, he must play out the game of life. His mother, Thetis, told him he would die at Troy, but stubborn Achilles preferred glorious battle to loss of pride.

Pride, the ancient Greeks believed, was man's fatal flaw.

Billy is destined to die in Fort Sumner, thought Rosa. He must keep his date with fate. Is it his pride that takes him there? Or is it honor? Both Achilles and Billy must uphold their honor, and only in war can true honor shine, so the warriors believe.

This is a violent time, a time of war and the warrior. The vaqueros on both sides believe they are warriors. Is Lincoln Troy?

I know the outline of Billy's history, Rosa reflected, but I cannot interfere in it. I feel like an alien in a foreign land, like Moses must have felt when he came out of Egypt. Oh, I feel close to the people. Their language, customs, and history are the same as mine. Some of these Mexicano families will move north along the Pecos River into the Puerto de Luna Valley and become part of my mother's history. Primos by marriage. The names tell the story: Chávez, Candelaria, Luna, Page, Gutiérrez, Mares, Campos, Baca, Romero, Sánchez, Ortega, González, the Bonneys of the Pastura llano, and on and on.

So why do I feel like an alien? Because this is not my time. I have been transported into a new song line—time itself has a meter, a rhythm. I feel it, but it is not mine. Is time simply a great harmony playing in the cosmos? Do harmonic vibrations explain how Billy got to Puerto de Luna, or how I got from there to here? A string symphony? Angelic violins? The old music of the spheres concept seems to fit the new string theory of the universe.

Somewhere I read about the idea of eternal recurrence. Life goes on repeating itself into infinity. The good, the bad, and the ugly repeat their lives. Am I in a recurring time? Was I here once before?

Rosa paused and looked down the dusty street. The Mexicanos of the village were going about their work, the men tending to their cattle or plowing fields for spring planting, the women heating water in huge cauldrons to wash the cotton mattress ticking. Spring cleaning, every house scrubbed clean of winter grime. Boys played marbles in rings scratched into the dirt, their dogs waiting patiently nearby. Girls played with their dolls. Any child past ten had been put to work. Childhood did not last long.

The children inquisitively paused to look at the woman who rode with Bilito. The woman from another time and place. "Buenos días," Rosa called.

They respectfully returned her buenos días.

The women stirring bars of homemade soap into the washtubs looked up, smiled, dried their hands on their aprons, and wondered who the young woman was who was staying at Josefa's. They knew she rode with Bilito and his vaqueros. But why would a young woman ride with the men?

They liked Bilito because he was respectful and spoke Spanish. He knew their ways, loved their bailes, wasn't condescending like other Americanos, but he was involved in the killings. The people were tired of the Dolans and McSweens. They wanted the streets to be safe for their children. They wanted to wash and hang clothes without fear of bullets flying. They wanted to go to their gardens in peace.

But war has come to Lincoln, thought Rosa, not because of a lovely Helen, but because men are set on acquiring power and wealth. If truth be told, that was true in the time of the *Iliad*. She remembered that the war against Troy had also been motivated by commercial interests. Troy stood on a bluff, from which it commanded the shipping lanes.

But Billy does not have the wrath of Achilles. He shows recklessness at times, but not rage. Does he really understand the bigger picture and believe he is in the right?

Rosa knocked on the door of Josefita Chávez's adobe. Josefita had invited her to coffee, and Rosa wondered why. Josefita, an Adelita if there ever was one, greeted Rosa and pulled her in. "We take care," she said, looking down the street before shutting the door. "Please sit. I have coffee."

Rosa said buenos días to the men at the table and sat down. Josefita poured her a cup of a thick black substance, coffee brewed with toasted flour, flavorful when sugar was added. "Estos son amigos," Josefita said, and Rosa again greeted the solemn-faced men who sat drinking coffee. She knew the men had been at the McSween home: Yginio Salazar, Francisco Zamora, José Chávez y Chávez, Ygnacio González, José María Sánchez, Florencio Chávez, Vicente Romero.

"You write books," Josefita said, and Rosa understood that this was why she had been invited.

"Yes."

"You write our story!" Josefita said. The stern woman Rosa had met on the ride to Seven Rivers was now passionate as she spoke. "Yes, we kill el Indio, but the newspaper not tell why. We lose our land. The Americanos want land for cattle. Soon all is lost."

"You ride with Billy to protect your land," Rosa said.

"Yes!" Josefita exclaimed. "All of us! In the book you write our names. Family names. We are the Españoles/Mexicanos who came from Méjico. Coronado came in 1540. Before us long ago. He knew this land. And de Vargas, also from Méjico."

"In newspaper only lies!" Chávez y Chávez stood and boomed out. Rosa knew this man was destined to play an interesting role in Billy's life. "We live here! El Bilito understand! In Santa Fe, los políticos want land. Ese Maxwell steal the land. Es un ladrón! We read el *New Mexican* paper. Governor Axtell, Catron, now the new sheriff, Peppin, all together bandidos!"

"But is McSween any better than Dolan? Don't they both want what they can get?"

The men nodded. Josefita sat and sipped her coffee.

"Yes, we know. We are mice, they are gatos. We try to save our land and feed our families."

Yginio stood. He was a tall man with a walrus mustache, a working rancher with hands and arms made of iron. He held his hat in his hands. "This is bad time. We want newspapers to know we fight for our land. Josefita speak for us." He nodded and sat down.

Josefita sketched out the story Rosa knew. The Navajos and Mescaleros had been corralled in Bosque Redondo, and their lands were up for grabs. Mexicano lands were also being taken, by hook or by crook. The Mexicanos had decided that the only way to save their land was to take up arms and fight on the side that might help them.

"You write in your book our story?" Josefita asked.

"Yes," Rosa said. "I will."

The men smiled and shook her hand. "Gracias, gracias."

"Que vayas con Dios," Josefita blessed her when Rosa was ready to leave.

An emotional meeting, Rosa thought as she walked back to Josefa's. Over a hundred years later, in my own time, the struggle to preserve the old Spanish and Mexican land grants is still being waged. The Atrisco and Tomé land grants will be lost to crooks. Josefita was begging her to write the history of the struggle, a struggle that would last into the next century. Rosa agreed, that is what she would write.

It was a battle for cultural survival, and the more Rosa learned, the more she understood that Billy was aware of the larger struggle. After all, the land issue was discussed by every Mexicano rancher or sheepherder he met. Maybe even during the dances with the young señoritas, they also spoke of the troubled times.

When they parted, Josefita had slipped Rosa a small, short-barreled pistol, a one-shot derringer. "You keep," she said. "For when you need. No se sabe cuando." Rosa felt the pistol in her pocket.

One never knows when one will need that one shot.

14

"Something on your mind, Rosa?"

"Just wondering . . ."

"I can feel it. I know all this is not easy on you."

"And you, Billy? How is it for you?"

"I don' know. I guess I'm doin' what I was meant to do. I love this country, the life of a vaquero. My dear mother used to say back east people were slaves. Living in tenements an' working for pennies. Here we're free. I din't mean to cross the law, but things work the way they work."

"Fate?"

"El destino, Ramón Bonney called it. We cain't prove it's there, an' we cain't prove otherwise. I feel I was meant to be here. In this time an' this place. The men I know are real compañeros. They stick by me an' I by them."

"Ride with them the rest of your life."

"No, expect not. Soon as all this is done, I want to get me a ranch. Maybe around Puerto de Luna. On the Pecos, the river I truly love."

"Go farther away—Mexico," Rosa suggested.

"I thought of that. Maybe with Abrana."

"Or maybe Sallie Chisum," Rosa teased.

Billy blushed and kicked dirt at his feet. "Ah, no, you been hearin' things. I've gone dancin' with her a few times, that's all. I'll head to Fort Sumner when all this is done."

Rosa shivered. There it was, his destiny pulling him to the town where he would die.

"Now come on, Rosa, I leveled with you. What's on your mind?"

"Saytir."

"Yeah, I been thinkin' on him. Why hasn't he made a move? You think he's gone? Gave up after Patas Grandes kicked the Himit's ass?"

"No, he's not gone, just waiting."

"Maybe he figures we humans will kill each other off an' he comes marchin' in. "

As good a prediction as any, thought Rosa. But Billy does not fully understand that Saytir and the Himits came from a future time. They used the wormhole on the river to get here. Just like Billy and me. Billy told Marcy he would protect me. Other than that, he has to lead his life to its tragic end.

"How did Saytir and those you call Himits get here? Does Marcy know?" Billy asked.

"Marcy did a lot of research. It was all in her computer. She hacked the C-Force computer, put everything on the flash drive. She figured out how we could time-travel through the wormhole. So when you came to help me, Saytir was able to transport himself and his Himit through the same wormhole."

"Whoa, hold on. I don' know what all that means. But I do know that thing you carry is dangerous. Marcy said that's what they want. So get rid of it. Bury it."

"Where?"

"It will come to you."

Rosa couldn't bury it. She had to get it back and have someone at Los Alamos Labs or Sandia Labs look at it. The genome formulas it contained were priceless scientific information.

"Where were you after Seven Rivers?"

"Up in the mountains. Nights we spent dancin' in San Patricio."

"You know Sheriff Peppin has a warrant for you?"

"Darned if every sumbitch in Lincoln County an' a few up in Santa Fe don' have a warrant for me. You don' see the politicos gettin' arrested, do you? They take care of each other. Now Peppin got Deputy José Chávez y Baca on his side. And recruited a few Mexicanos who should know better. He aims to split the Mexicanos here, make 'em fight each other. We got Martín Chávez from Picacho on our side—"

"Billy!" someone called, and Billy spun like a cougar, in the same motion drawing his pistol.

"Tom? You aim to get shot?"

"Sorry I came up like that, but Peppin and Dolan got a posse together. They be riding to Lincoln!"

"Pues, vamoose!" Billy called, and hurried to the corral. The Regulators saddled up and rode into Lincoln, hoping to beat the Dolan posse. They slipped quietly into the town and took up positions. Billy insisted that Rosa hide in the McSween home. "It's the safest," he said.

No place seemed safe that afternoon of July 15 when Dolan's posse rode into Lincoln and was greeted by a barrage of gunfire from the Regulators.

Rosa peered out a window and took notes: "The Battle of Lincoln has begun. A few days ago, or seconds if all this is a dream, I was writing about the Lincoln gunfight in my novel, and now here I am." She described the sharp report of the rifles, the painful shrieking cry of a horse as it fell, the curses of Dolan's men as they ran for cover, the smell of gunpowder. After the initial confrontation, an eerie silence descended as the sides settled down to analyze the situation.

"Come away from the window," Sue McSween cautioned Rosa. "You might get hurt."

Rosa wondered again if she could die in time past; she was from time future. No sense in finding out, she thought.

"I fear this terrible outburst is going to last," Sue continued. "My husband and I are prisoners in our own home."

To keep busy and stay out of the way, Rosa helped Sue in the kitchen. That evening she packed supper for the men and ran to the Ellis store, where a group of Regulators had taken position. Billy complimented her. "Hey, Tom, ain't she brave. You might take a likin' to her."

Tom O'Folliard blushed. "Ain't got time," he whispered, thinking, Sure would like to.

The sporadic gunfight continued for four days, with neither side getting the upper hand. A few citizens complained to Colonel

Nathan Dudley at Fort Stanton, and finally he entered Lincoln, leading the black Ninth Cavalry into town. He proceeded to make camp but did not interfere.

Sue McSween watched the soldiers bivouac and swore. "Enough is enough. My nerves are frayed, my husband refuses to move out, and the soldiers sit and do nothing." She grabbed a bonnet, left the house, and marched down the street. She cornered Sheriff Peppin and berated him for his cowardice, then proceeded to the army camp to do the same to Colonel Dudley. All to no avail. The Ninth Cavalry pulled out of range.

"Stupid men," she said on returning. Thankfully, no one had taken a potshot at the angry woman.

On the fifth day, when Rosa awoke, she heard window shutters being blasted open. She watched as Dolan's posse got close enough to the McSween house for Deputy Turner to shout that he had a warrant for McSween. "I won't surrender to you!" a defiant McSween called back, and the standoff continued.

During the four days Billy had stayed busy, running back and forth to the various positions the Regulators had taken. That afternoon he spotted a man with a torch behind the house. "Andy's got fire!" he shouted, but too late. Andy Boyle had just set fire to the McSween house. The house was built of adobe, and the fire spread slowly, first burning vigas and ceilings as it spread from room to room. From their vantage point, the Dolanites could clearly see anyone attempting to put out the blaze.

"It's time to move out," Billy shouted. He had tried to persuade a distraught McSween to leave, but the man who was once in command was now incapable of making a decision.

"I will not run like a coward," McSween insisted, clutching a Bible and shouting, "The righteous will be saved!"

"Then I got to save Rosa," Billy said, dashing into the kitchen and grabbing her. "McSween don' know what to do. Sue an' her sister are escapin'. Best for us to do the same!"

With the flames licking the night sky, José Chávez y Chávez, Tom

O'Folliard, Jim French, Harvey Morris, and Billy and Rosa made their way out the back door. Morris caught a bullet and went down in front of Rosa. "Lord!" he cried. Rosa stopped to help.

"Come away, Rosa," Billy said. "Listen."

They heard McSween shout, "I surrender! I surrender!"

"Stay put, Rosa. We'll get Harvey out."

"My laptop," Rosa cried. She had left it on the kitchen table. Without hesitation, she jumped up and ran back to the smoke-filled house. She entered the kitchen through a back door and felt her way along a wall.

"Thank God," she whispered. She grabbed the computer and started out.

Flames and smoke licking at a doorway revealed a priest.

"Father?"

"No, not a holy man," the priest answered.

"Saytir!"

"None other. The laptop," he growled. "Give it up."

Rosa leaped toward the door, but Saytir struck quickly. His blow sent her sprawling to the floor. Around them the blazing fire was spreading, an inferno only feet away.

"You fooled me once, but not again!" Saytir shouted above the crackling flames. A viga in the living area fell with a loud crash; the entire roof was about to collapse.

Rosa's head spun. She clutched the laptop. If the beast got hold of the flash drive, the earth would become a living hell.

"It's over," Saytir gloated, ready to strike again.

"Not yet," Rosa replied, reaching into her leather jacket for the pistol Josefita had given her. She cocked the derringer and fired into Saytir's eyes.

"Damn you!" the monster cried, falling back. It had not expected Rosa to be armed.

From somewhere in the smoke-filled kitchen, Rosa heard Billy call her name.

"Saytir!" she cried.

"Get back!" Billy shouted. He whipped out his pistol and fired six quick shots at Saytir. The Himit toppled back into the roaring inferno.

Billy grabbed Rosa, and together they ran out the back door just as the entire roof crashed to the ground, flames and sparks lighting up the night sky.

15

The following morning, they learned that Robert Beckwith and three men had entered the house and opened fire on McSween. Beckwith was killed. Five bullets hit McSween, who fell dead. Of the Regulators, Francisco Zamora and Vicente Romero were killed. Yginio Salazar was wounded but escaped along with José María Chávez and Florencio Chávez.

McSween was buried the following morning. His wife, Chisum, a few Mexicano ranchers, and some citizens gathered at the gravesite. From where she stood, Rosa could hear the minister intoning the Sermon on the Mount. "Blessed are they that mourn, for they shall be comforted. Blessed are the meek, for they shall inherit the earth . . . the peacemakers . . ."

Peace, wondered Rosa. In my time, wars are raging in Iraq, Afghanistan, Syria, and the West Bank, and Iran and North Korea are seeking nuclear bombs. Ethnic cleansing in Darfur, children starving in Sudan, and here Lincoln County was at war. She knew how this one would end.

Yginio Salazar, she learned, had crawled to the nearby house of a friend, where he was tended to. So he was alive. This man was one of the most interesting of the vaqueros. He always seemed to be in the action, and it was clear he admired Billy. But there was no biography of Yginio, and only historical footnotes here and there. Maybe when she finished her novel about Billy, she would have some time to gather some information about him.

The Lincoln County Mexicanos' history had not yet been written. In spite of many obstacles, they had settled the Pecos River and the Río Bonito valleys. They farmed, ran cattle and sheep, built a church, and started a school for the children. Family life was important to the Mexicanos.

The bodies of Vicente Romero and Francisco Zamora had been

returned to their respective homes and laid in hastily constructed wood coffins. Today they would be buried. "Terrible night," Josefa moaned as she and Rosa made their way to Vicente's home to console his widow. The previous night Josefa had cooked a large batch of red chile enchiladas, and Rosa had made a pile of tortillas. They carried the food to the Romero house. Martín's offering was a bottle of wine.

Smoke still rose from the McSween home. Townspeople moved up and down the dirt street, on their way to offer condolences and assistance. Families from nearby ranches rode in on buckboards, men on horseback.

The news of the battle had spread down the river as far as Picacho and north to Capitán. A priest, Father Sambrano, was visiting in Tularosa, and that night two men had been sent to bring him to officiate at the burials. "Father Lassaigne was our priest," Josefa said. "He did mass, baptize, marry people. We have one morada at Placita de Gendres. Oratorio de San José. Capilla de San Patricio. Nuestra Señora del Pueblito. Now Father Sambrano. He was born Arroyo Seco, you know. Imagine, he study with Padre Martínez from Taos. A good priest. Algún día we finish church here for Lincoln." Everyone knew the story of Padre Martínez from Taos and his excommunication by Bishop Lamy. A fascinating story of church history in New Mexico.

"Are there penitentes here?" Rosa asked.

"Sí. They take care of funeral today. They help mucho."

They entered the small adobe home, and Josefa introduced Rosa to Vicente's widow. Rosa and Josefa offered their condolences and sat with the family. Martín stayed outside with the men gathered there. All morning and into the early afternoon, visitors entered and passed by the coffin to pay their last respects. The penitentes prayed a rosary and sang what Rosa thought were the most mournful alabados she had ever heard.

The praying went on, mixed with talk of the killing, interrupted by the noon meal. The women of the village had quickly organized, delivering large bowls of beans, posole, carne seca cooked in red chile, and tortillas. Two large coffee pots had to be filled over and over as the guests ate and washed down the tasty food with coffee. A meal for the dead men, a parting.

This was the velorio, the wake, a tradition. The food provided strength for the long walk to the cemetery. There would be a few descansos along the way where the priest would pause to pray. At each descanso the mourners would pause to remember the departed, then slowly trudge on to the cemetery.

In the whispered conversations, Rosa heard anger. "McSween was a good man. Honest."

"The pinche Murphys y Dolans kill him. El sharife Peppin is with them."

"Están todos juntos."

"Una bola de cabrones."

"Y también Catron y los de Santa Fe!"

"Vicente y Francisco muertos, ¿y por qué?"

"You think Santa Fe will take care of their children? Don't even think it."

The people knew the five-day Battle of Lincoln had been fought because opposing economic and political forces were seeking control of the territory. The Americanos from los Estados Unidos were moving in to claim Hispanic and Indian land. Already many of the Mescaleros had been removed to Bosque Redondo. Were the Mexicanos next?

Late in the afternoon, Father Sambrano arrived. None too soon, Rosa thought, for July 20, 1878, was a scorching day. The priest said a prayer and sprinkled holy water; then the men hefted the coffins onto their shoulders and headed for the camposanto. The mourners followed, women in black grieving for the dead men, comforting the widows. The men, most having taken a few drinks of the homemade whiskey called mula, were somber.

As they neared the cemetery, a solemn Billy appeared and joined Rosa. He would take his chances with the sheriff to see his friends buried. "Billy," Rosa whispered and took his arm. "I'm glad to see you. Are you all right?"

Josefa smiled. "Bilito. Gracias a Dios."

All in the crowd were glad to see that Billy had survived.

The five-day battle and sleeping in the hills that night had taken a toll on Billy. He looked tired, and for the first time Rosa noted sadness in his eyes. The deaths of his friends were also weighing heavily on the spirited young man.

At the graves, the priest spoke of the need to end the violence and turn to the guidance of the church.

Over Sierra Blanca, towering cumulus clouds had been forming. July thunderstorms were common on the llano, turning the dry earth into mud, but welcomed by the people as blessing rain. Grass would green for the animals.

The mourners stood with heads bowed as the priest finished his comments. "We are made of mud, and to mud we return," he intoned, adding, "la vida es un sueño," a quote from a favorite Spanish playwright. "Que descanse en paz."

Everyone made the sign of the cross, including Billy. Rosa looked surprised. "My good mother taught me a few prayers," he said. "La Virgen de Guadalupe saved my skin a few times. A curandera in Saltillo gave me the Virgin's scapular."

On their way to Josefa's, the priest turned to Rosa. "I hear you ride with the vaqueros. They say you carry a strange, magical box."

"A laptop," Rosa said. It was a magical box to those who did not know about computers. "It was a gift from my father."

"I see. Well, the people love to make up stories. I myself do not believe in witchcraft."

Laptops as witchcraft? Rosa had to smile.

"You sure are good with that toy pistol," Billy teased.

"I think I'll keep it," Rosa replied. "If you'll reload it for me."

"I should teach you how to use one of these six-shooters."

"I think I'll keep this. And thanks for saving my life."

"You took care of yourself, alright. I think Saytir will be hurtin' a lot from those bullets he has to take out of his hide."

84

"The bullets didn't kill him?"

"Nah. Saytir's not a regular Himit. Bullets cain't penetrate his body armor. Difficult beast to kill."

"But the burning roof fell on him."

"He made his way out alright."

"Why was he dressed as a priest?"

"He likes disguises, I guess. Remember, he was a sheriff on the bridge."

A playful beast? Rosa felt confused.

The burial done, the mourners returned to their homes. Josefa had food left over from the velorio. Billy ate enough for three men. "With bullets flying, my appetite was slim," he laughed.

"You have special saint," Martín said. "Five days you run here, there. Bullets like angry hornets, pero no one hit you. ¡Viva Bilito!"

They raised their coffee cups in salute.

"We live in violent times," Father Sambrano said. "The violence comes because the law has broken down. In Santa Fe the big políticos who desire wealth pull the strings. Look at what Lucien Maxwell has done up north. He has stolen so many land grants that he now owns half of Río Arriba. Two million acres."

"The crooks de Santa Fe Ring help the ladrón," Josefa said.

The priest nodded. "Dolan, Murphy, and their partner, John Riley, own the legislature. All crooks, including Thomas Catron, the U.S. district attorney for the territory, and Governor Axtell. Even the clerk of the district court is involved. They know the law and use it to steal Spanish land grants and Indian land. When evil men use the law to get rich, everyone suffers. God help us."

Those gathered around Josefa's table nodded assent.

Rosa thought of C-Force sitting in the Oval Office, advising the president. Evil men getting richer and more powerful, all on the backs of the people.

16

Billy and the Regulators vanished into the hills. The Battle of Lincoln was over, but as Josefa cautioned, "Dolan bandidos try get Bilito. They get false warrant for Bilito."

She and Rosa had heated water early that morning and taken it out to the big washtub near the corral. The sudsy water splashed over the sides of the cajete to the rhythm of Josefa's strong strokes on the washboard. Every single piece of clothing was thoroughly washed.

Spic 'n' span, Rosa thought as she rinsed and hung the laundry on the clothesline near the house. It will take all day to do the wash. With my washer and dryer, I would be done in—she dropped the thought. I'm here, not there.

Some shearers had come the day before and sheared Martín's sheep. He and his young helper had departed early that morning to drive the sheep closer to the mountain meadows. The boy and his dog would stay with the herd all summer.

"What will happen now?" asked Rosa.

"Father Sambrano say, the Santa Fe Ring is rotten. Políticos want our land. They mine for gold. Now Presbyterians come." She whispered, "You know, they do not pray to la Virgen."

"Billy carries her scapular."

"Bilito is good boy. Where did you meet Bilito?"

In another time, thought Rosa. "In Puerto de Luna."

"Puerto de Luna. We go there. Muy bonito. Mucha manzana, durazno, maíz, chile verde. Bilito go there. I think he have querida, the sister of Liborio Mares."

"Yes, he told me he likes to dance with Liborio's sister. Does Billy go to mass?"

"No sé. Pero Irish son católicos, ¿qué no? Bishop Lamy come visit to Fort Stanton. I think twelve year ago. We want a church, but he say no. I don' like ese Lamy—¡Mira! ¡Bilito!"

"In a hurry," Rosa said as Billy came riding up.

"Buenos días," he called. "Sorry to interrupt your work, ladies, but we got to ride."

"¿Qué pasa?" Josefa asked.

"Sheriff Peppin and Dolan may be comin' this way. Best to get out of town."

"Ay, Dios, always problems. Go, Rosa. I finish."

While she saddled Mancita, Billy explained, "We was at the Indian agency. Atanacio Martínez shot Bernstein. The dumb clerk rode into a gunfight an' got killed. Sure as the vulture stinks, they're gonna pin it on me."

"Where to?" Rosa asked.

"John Chisum's brothers are runnin' some cattle to Fort Sumner. We can ride along if you're willin'."

Rosa nodded, wondering if riding north on the Pecos meant they might cross paths with Pat Garrett. Or Saytir. Within hours they met up with the Chisum herd and rode north across the wide and wind-swept Llano Estacado. The only sign of life was the cloud of dust the herd raised, the lowing of the cows, and the vultures gliding over-head. They occasionally spotted a coyote chasing a jackrabbit.

The Nuevo Mexicanos in Fort Sumner welcomed Billy and friends by throwing a dance. Billy danced all night with Abrana. At one point the master of ceremonies, the bastonero, announced a valse chiquiao. He placed a chair in the middle of the floor, and everyone cheered when he looked at Billy and Abrana and addressed them with a verse while the musicians played a slow waltz.

> De estos dos que andan bailando
> si mi vista no me engaña,
> anda bailando la reina
> con el príncipe de España.*

---

*Of these two who are dancing
 if my eyes do not deceive me,
 the queen is dancing
 with the prince of Spain.

Then he asked Abrana to sit in the chair. "Now, Billy, you must get her to dance with you."

Billy knew verses to the song, but could he sing one that would get Abrana to dance? If he did, the dance could continue.

Rosa and Abrana looked worried. So did the other dancers who were looking on. Billy smiled, took Abrana's hand, and sang:

> Eres bella como el sol
> hermosa como la luna;
> hay estrellas en el cielo
> pero como tú ninguna.†

Abrana rose, and Billy swept her off in a waltz. Everyone cheered, and the dance continued.

The next day they rode on to Puerto de Luna, again enjoying the good food of friends and the prescribed nightly dance. Then on to Anton Chico, a small hamlet on the Pecos River. That night the festivities were interrupted by the appearance of the San Miguel County sheriff, Desiderio Romero. He had learned that Billy was in the vicinity, and he had a warrant for his arrest. He rode in from Las Vegas with eight deputies. They entered Manuel Sánchez's saloon ready for action.

Rosa watched as Billy and the vaqueros turned to meet them. The musicians stopped playing. The guitar and violin, which moments earlier were squeaking out a hot polka, suddenly went dead.

Dressed in a vaquero outfit with a sombrero pulled over her eyes, Rosa sat quietly in a dark corner. She had grown good at *disappearing*. Disappearing meant she could blend into the background. Soon those around her didn't even notice she was there.

At times like that, she wondered if she could *really* affect the time

---

†You are as beautiful as the sun
 lovely as the moon;
 of all the stars in heaven
 none can compare to you.

warp she was caught in. Could she disappear out of this time and back to her house in Puerto de Luna? Could she find herself reading and making notes, perhaps calling Bobby in LA, telling him she missed him? Calling her parents in Santa Fe?

Some believe a person can levitate by willing it. Some can hypnotize themselves. If that was true, and this is what intrigued Rosa, then perhaps she could create a wormhole by practicing deep meditation. Were there other ways to make wormholes? Not just a wormhole created when a supernova exploded, but something like the one at the Puerto de Luna Bridge.

She had gotten so good at disappearing that often Billy and the vaqueros seemed not to be aware of her. At the Puerto de Luna saloon, she had fallen asleep at the table, and after the dance they had departed without her. They forgot she was there. She used to ride next to Billy; now more and more she trailed in the back in the dust the horses raised.

That's how it had been on the trail to Fort Sumner. Dust and an empty landscape, with gigantic clouds rising into the blue sky in the late afternoons. The Cloud People of the Mescaleros, cumulus cotton clouds with dark underbellies, dazzling with vibrant splashes of color. Thunderstorms struck, and the buffalo trails the herd was following turned into mud. The cowboys cursed and moved on. Late in the afternoon they stopped to make camp.

The camp cook brewed a large pot of coffee that quickly had to be replenished. He cooked a carne seca stew with potatoes and dry green chile pods. Warmed-over tortillas and hardtack biscuits completed the satisfying meal.

That evening he made a space in the chuck wagon where Rosa could sleep. In the dark she wrote a note on her laptop. She was thinking of home. "This is not home," she wrote, "this is more like hell." She quickly erased the negative entry. She was here because of her desire to write Billy's true story. Had she sold her soul to the devil in exchange for it? She felt like crying. Where was home? How could she return?

Now she watched as Billy threw down the gauntlet. "Sheriff," he said, "why don' you an' your deputies have a drink with us. If you throw down on us, we're goin' to get Manuel's saloon messy. Besides, there's innocent people here, just enjoyin' the baile." He flashed his disarming smile, left hand resting on his pistol.

Each side was armed to the teeth. Each side glared at the other. Rosa held her breath. Any false move would set off a gunfight in which there would be no winners.

The sheriff studied the situation and knew he couldn't win. The Kid was right. "Okay, William Bonney. Maybe I arrest you next time. Anden, muchachos, tomamos un trago y nos vamos." The deputies drank down the whiskeys the bartender poured, and then they exited and rode out of Anton Chico, leaving Billy and the rest to finish enjoying the night's dance.

"Glad you stayed with the horses," Billy told Rosa the following morning. "Sheriff Romero was ready to draw down."

She hadn't stayed with the horses. She had been right there in the saloon, but he hadn't seen her.

The following week, they headed up to the Texas Panhandle to sell stolen horses to Texans running large cattle herds on the grassy Llano Estacado. Billy was now the leader of the dwindling group of Regulators. That autumn, only he, Tom O'Folliard, and Rosa headed back to Fort Sumner. Always Fort Sumner, Rosa noted. Was it to spend time with Abrana, or was fate drawing him like a magnet? After a short visit, though, he wanted to ride on. Rosa could tell that he was restless. Even Abrana could not get him to stay.

One evening in late November, Billy rushed up to Rosa with a big grin on his face. "There's great news!" he exclaimed. "I'm tol' that President Hayes made Lew Wallace governor of the New Mexico Territory, an' Wallace has issued us a pardon. They say it was printed in the newspapers. An' we got a new sheriff, George Kimbrell."

"That's wonderful, Billy! What now?"

"No more hidin', Rosa. No more lookin' over our shoulders all the time. Glory be, we are free at last," he said, dancing around the room.

So two weeks later, a newly upbeat Billy and Rosa rode back to Lincoln—another magnet waiting with its own tragic consequences.

17

But back in Lincoln, the news they heard was different: Billy was told that the pardon did not apply to him. "Is it true?" he asked Rosa, handing her a copy of the *New Mexican* newspaper in which the proclamation had been published. Rosa read it carefully. It said that the governor had issued "a general pardon for misdemeanors and offenses committed in the said County of Lincoln . . . to persons who at the time of the commission of the offenses and misdemeanors of which they may be accused were with good intent, residents of the said Territory, and who should hereafter have kept the peace and conducted themselves in all respects as becomes good citizens." However, it would not be extended to "any person in bar of conviction under indictment now found and returned for any such crimes or misdemeanors, nor . . . any party undergoing pains and penalties consequent upon sentence heretofore had for any crime or misdemeanor."

"Yes, it's true," said Rosa, looking at Billy. "It says that the pardon is only good if you don't have any indictments. And you have two: one for the murder of Sheriff Brady and one for the murder of Buckshot Roberts."

"Ah, don' you worry 'bout the fine print," said Billy. "I can prove I warn't the only one in those gunfights. They pinned all those flyin' bullets on me? I know Jesse Evans an' Billy Campbell want me dead. Maybe Wallace is an honest man." He was sure the governor would include him in the pardon and things would get better. He would soon be able to head down to Mexico with Abrana, buy a ranch, and live the life of a free man.

Rosa felt a growing sense of unease. Not just because she knew where Billy's life was headed, but also because Saytir had not made another appearance. Where was he and what was he up to? Why hadn't he made another attempt to get the flash drive? Maybe it isn't valuable after all, thought Rosa. Could C-Force, working with Saytir, reconstruct the genome formulas? Create more Himits? If the president ordered C-Force to create a Himit army, the world would be doomed. That's what Marcy had told Rosa. He didn't need to hit the nuclear button to erase North Korea's arsenal; all he needed was Saytir and an army of super-monsters.

How can I get this message back home? she wondered. How did I get into this mess? Why am I here? The existential question. Isn't it more important to be back home? I want to finish my novel, get married, have kids, go back to my teaching job at Cal State, enjoy literary discussions with my colleague Roberto Cantú. Buy my grandparents a home in Puerto de Luna, spend summers writing. Maybe Bobby could quit his job and become a small-town sheriff. Quit making foolish plans! she scolded herself. She had no idea when or how she'd be able to return to real time.

Despite Billy's optimism, there had been no offer of amnesty by spring, and with the indictments against him still in force, he decided to try writing to Governor Wallace. He showed Rosa the letter before he sent it:

March 13, 1879

To his Excellency the Governor
General Lew Wallace

Dear Sir, I have heard that You will give one thousand $ dollars
for my body which as I can understand it means alive as a
witness. I know it is as a witness against those that murdered
Mr. Chapman. if it was so as that I could appear at Court I
could give the desired information, but I have indictments
against me for things that happened in the late Lincoln County
War and am afraid to give up because my Enemies would Kill
me. the day Mr. Chapman was murdered I was in Lincoln, at
the request of good Citizens to meet Mr. J.J. Dolan to meet as
Friends, so as to be able to lay aside our arms and go to Work.

I was present when Mr. Chapman was murdered and know
who did it and if it were not for those indictments I would have
made it clear before now. if it is in your power to Annully those
indictments I hope you will do so so as to give me a chance to
explain. Please send me an awnser telling me what you can do
You can send awnser by bearer I have no wish to fight any more
indeed I have not raised an arm since your proclamation. As
to my character I refer to any of the citizens, for the majority of
them are my friends and have been helping me all they could.
I am called Kid Antrim but Antrim is my stepfathers name.
    Waiting for an awnser I remain your Obedeint Servant
                                                    W. H. Bonney

"What do you think?" Billy asked.

"It's worth a shot," she agreed.

Governor Wallace was under public pressure to corral the violence
in Lincoln County. He had ordered the new captain at Fort Stanton to
put every renegade in jail, but he was willing to meet with Billy. He
wrote back:

Lincoln, March 15, 1879

W. H. Bonney,

Come to the house of Squire Wilson (not the lawyer) at nine o'clock
next Monday night alone. I don't mean his office, but his residence.
Follow along the foot of the mountain south of the town, come in
on that side, and knock on the east door. I have authority to exempt
you from prosecution, if you will testify to what you say you know.

    The object of the meeting at Squire Wilson's is to arrange the
matter in a way to make your life safe. To do that the utmost
secrecy is to be used. So come along. Don't tell anybody—not a
living soul—where you are coming or the object. If you could trust
Jesse Evans, you can trust me.

                                                    Lew Wallace

It's a scene worthy of a western movie, thought Rosa as they made their way to Squire Wilson's simple home near the Lincoln courthouse on that cold, blustery night. She clutched her laptop. Here I am, ready to record conversations lost to time. The Arrow of Time can work for you or against you.

Billy knocked on the door. Squire Wilson opened it and beckoned them in.

"Is the governor here?" a wary Billy asked.

"Who is it?" the governor asked.

Billy stepped forward. "Soy Billy Bonney. Some call me Kid Antrim, but Antrim is my stepfather's name."

The coal oil lantern on the table illuminated Wallace as he stood to greet Billy. "You have caused me grief," he said.

"An' grief has been paid to me," Billy answered.

"Who is with you?"

"A friend. She's gonna write my life story."

"What are you carrying, young lady?" the cautious governor inquired.

"A box," Rosa replied and sank back into the shadows. "Writing papers."

"Humph!" Wallace turned to Billy. "Now let's get down to business. If you testify before the grand jury and the trial court convicts the murderers of Mr. Chapman, I will let you go scot-free with a pardon in your pocket for all your past misdeeds."

What seemed like a great bargain had problems for Billy. He had agreed with the Dolan gang not to testify against Chapman's killers. During a drunken brawl, the Dolan cowboys had shot the man for no good reason.

"Hold on," Billy cautioned, resting his Winchester on the table. "If I testify against Jesse Evans and Billy Campbell, they will kill me."

Wallace thought a moment. "We can arrange a sham arrest," he suggested. "Put you in jail and protect you till trial." He explained the plan, and the night ended with an agreement in place.

Four days later, Sheriff Kimbrell arrested Billy and Tom O'Folliard.

Rosa watched as they were placed under guard in the Juan Patrón home.

But the agreement didn't hold. District Attorney William Rynerson hated Billy and had vowed to try him for the murder of Sheriff Brady and Buckshot Roberts. Billy appealed to Governor Wallace, but he would not interfere in the matter.

"The governor reneged," Billy swore. "Time to ride."

"Where to?"

"Las Vegas. The best gambling goin' on in the state. A poor boy's got to earn a livin'."

They bribed the guard, and in the dark of night they rode out of Lincoln.

On July 4, 1879, Rosa, Billy, and Tom found themselves in the midst of a tumultuous crowd filling the streets of Las Vegas, New Mexico. The town was celebrating the arrival of the first Santa Fe Railway train. Whiskey flowed freely, gunshots rang, musicians composed corridos on the spot, dancing filled the streets, children and barking dogs ran wild, and the saloons were filled to the brim.

"Of such events is history made," Rosa typed into the Billy the Kid file on her laptop. But will New Mexicans remember this date and the train's arrival? Or does the Arrow of Time eventually erase all events? You can't trust people's memory. The grandchildren of these hardy Nuevo Mexicanos will not know the importance of this date. Nor will they know that Jesse James was in town and exchanged greetings with Billy. Who will remember? Or care? That meeting between Jesse James and Billy would make a very interesting novel, or a movie. Who would write it? Maybe Max Evans, except that the old cowboy writer was getting up in age.

A few days later Sheriff Romero showed up, playing the part of a considerate lawman. He and his heavily armed deputies approached Billy cautiously. "Get out of my jurisdiction, Kid, and I won't arrest you."

Billy knew better than to draw on the sheriff. "Bueno, sharife. Ya me voy. Party's over. We'll mosey on to Fort Sumner. The law's not so stiff there."

He laughed all the way to the livery stable, where they saddled up and rode south. Fort Sumner was a lawless town. The saloons were filled to the brim, and the weekend bailes drew pretty girls from Santa Rosa, Anton Chico, Puerto de Luna, and the ranches within a ten-mile radius.

Billy gambled in the saloons, but more lucrative employment was rustling Texas Panhandle cattle and selling them through a middleman to the Mescalero Agency or to the miners in White Oaks. Demand for beef was high. Billy and his friends drove their "found" herds down to Los Portales and sold them there to crooked buyers.

With time on her hands, Rosa interviewed some of the young women who were connected to Billy. Every small town along the Pecos seemed to be home to a young woman bragging that she was Billy's true querida. There were quite a few women in Billy's life, as Rosa found out. She made a list.

1. Paulita, Pete (Pedro) Maxwell's sister, who said Billy was always smiling and good-natured, very polite, and danced remarkably well. Was she a querida? Perhaps Billy had not paid her enough attention. Billy's fateful day will take place July 14, 1881, in Pete Maxwell's Fort Sumner home. Paulita will be there.
2. Nasaria, Tom Yerby's wife, who some said had a daughter fathered by Billy.
3. Celsa Gutiérrez, whose sister was married to Pat Garrett, the man who would kill Billy.
4. Abrana García, Billy's querida.
5. Sallie Chisum, who was a romance, but the details were sketchy.
6. Were there others? Names lost to the Arrow of Time.

The Mexicana beauties loved to dance with Billy. He was respectful, and he always bathed before a dance, unlike the other vaqueros. Those young ladies swooned when he smiled, and some later made up stories about nonexistent romantic interludes. Young and full of fun, a good dancer when bailes were about the only form of entertainment in the Pecos River villages, and having acquired the reputation of a vaquero who sided with the poor Mexicanos, Billy attracted the young women.

Why not, Rosa noted. The last Hollywood Billy the Kid movie she had seen cast only Sallie Chisum as one of Billy's queridas. The writer and director didn't mention Abrana. Except for one dark cowboy with a Spanish accent, the Mexicanos were kept in the background. Movie extras.

What a great novel the loves in Billy's life would make. Cyrano of the Pecos. Maybe that's what I should be writing, thought Rosa. But one had to separate the truth from wishful thinking and fantasies. Billy danced with them all, and many a lovely young woman began to think she was the chosen one. But Billy kept his freedom.

Billy had friends in every town along the Pecos, and Rosa was always welcomed as a guest. At first families greeted her as Billy's girlfriend, his querida who rode with him, but soon la gente realized the relationship was not a love affair.

"They do not sleep together," the elders would whisper when alone.

"He stays with the vaqueros."

"But she is welcome here."

"Sí, any friend of Bilito is our friend."

"Maybe she is like Josefita Chávez. In Lincoln County she rides with the vaqueros. They say she killed a man."

The women smiled. "It is time we show the men we can shoot."

Rosa recorded the names of the families she met in the Pecos River villages. They always welcomed her into their homes, gave her a place to sleep, shared their meals. The women were the strength of the family and community. Work was strenuous and difficult for the men outdoors, and just as hard for the women. Raising families, preparing meals, canning for winter, making soap from lard and lye, washing, sewing, gardening, sometimes riding to the range to help with shearing sheep or branding cattle, bringing in water from cisterns or the river, chopping wood, cooking three meals on a wood-burning stove, attending church, raising chickens, having babies, curing every conceivable illness that struck family or neighbors, helping their comadres: the list was endless and exhausting.

Rosa helped with chores. She enjoyed the company of the women and the children who were always nearby, helping. From riding and from work, she felt she had grown stronger. Would she become a Josefita and decide to carry a pistol? Be capable of shooting Saytir again?

"The women of strong arms and strong backs," she wrote. Here's another book begging to be written. I'll record the names of these Mexicanas who keep their families well-fed, clothed, and together. For a moment she thought she should write their story. Don't get sidetracked, she told herself. Keep with Billy's story.

Maybe CiCi could tell the women's story. She could present the idea to RC at the OU Press and get a contract for the book. I'll send her everything! Information no one else has ever recorded! Details! Names! Emotions! An encyclopedia of facts about the true life of Billy the Kid!

Rosa punched SEND, but it would not go. "Darn," she said to herself. "I'll try later."

18

There were many stories to record. The plight of the Mescalero Apaches of the area touched Rosa. Perhaps the story began with Colonel James H. Carleton. In 1862 he marched the California Column, an army of two thousand men, from California to New Mexico. He was charged with driving Sibley's Confederate Army out of New Mexico. But Sibley had already lost to Union forces and was gone by the time Carleton arrived.

General Carleton was named the commander of the Department of New Mexico, headquartered in Santa Fe. His first order of business was to control and punish the Mescalero Apaches. In late 1862 he ordered Fort Stanton to be reoccupied, and he sent Colonel Kit Carson to punish the recent aggressions of the Mescaleros.

Rosa read Carleton's instructions to Carson: "All Indian men of [the Mescalero] tribe are to be killed whenever and wherever you can find them. The women and children will not be harmed, but you will take them prisoners, and feed them at Fort Stanton until you receive other instructions about them . . . we believe if we kill some of their men in fair, open war, they will be apt to remember that it will be better for them to remain at peace than to be at war."

The letter made Rosa's blood run cold. A time of dread and fear had descended on the territory. Payback time meant that for a few raids young Mescaleros had conducted against the Anglo and Mexicano homesteaders, the entire tribe was to suffer.

Carleton wrote to Carson: "There is to be no council held with the Indians, nor any talks. The men are to be slain whenever and wherever they can be found. The women and children may be taken as prisoners, but, of course, they are not to be killed. . . . They have robbed and murdered the people with impunity too long already."

Kit Carson hunted all the Mescaleros within a hundred-mile radius of Fort Stanton, killing thirty-two along with Chief José Largo.

The rest were marched to Bosque Redondo, the concentration camp on the Pecos River near the fateful town of Fort Sumner.

Carleton had an underlying motive: with the Mescaleros and Gila Apaches out of the way, Anglo miners could mine historically Indian lands for gold and other precious metals. The Gila Apaches were to be taken "prisoners of war," and once they were subdued, "the Pino Alto gold mines can then be worked with security . . . whose development will tend greatly to the prosperity of this Territory."

Manifest destiny at work. Manifest destiny at its worst.

Prosperity at the price of imprisoning a people. In the fall of 1862 and into 1863, many Gila Apaches were killed. Their chief, Mangas Colorado, was lured into consultation with the soldiers and killed in cold blood.

Rosa shivered. Is this the Law of the West? A false law created by those full of greed for gold and land. The land that once belonged to the Gila and Mescalero Apaches was filling with settlers.

There were good people in the territory opposed to the general's inhumane orders. The death of Mangas Colorado stirred public sentiment against Carleton, but in the East the country was fighting a civil war, and there was little opposition in Washington to his plan.

The Mescaleros were rounded up and settled in Bosque Redondo, one of the worst tracts of land along the Pecos River. The water was alkaline, and the land was poor for farming. Carleton then turned his efforts against the Navajos, who for the past two centuries had terrorized both Pueblo Indian and Hispano settlements along the northern Río Grande. On April 14, 1863, the First Regiment New Mexico Volunteers under the command of Colonel Kit Carson marched against the Navajos.

Carson burned the Navajos' peach orchards and cornfields and confiscated their sheep. He starved them into submission, so that by March of 1864 he had over eight thousand Navajo prisoners ready to march from Canyon de Chelly country to Bosque Redondo. The infamous Long Walk to Fort Sumner had begun. Herding them in small groups, it took two or three years to get the Navajos to Bosque

Redondo. By the time they reached the Pecos River, hundreds had died along the way from hunger, disease, and freezing March snowstorms.

Many died of heartache, Rosa wrote. To leave their homeland was considered taboo. Enclosed by mountains sacred to the Navajos, the country they had occupied was their birthright. We emerged from this earth, their legends told. We are of this earth.

The experiment was a disaster. The Mescaleros felt overwhelmed by the Navajos. The hail and freezing rain storms of 1865 ruined crops throughout the territory. By late 1865, the starving Mescaleros fled Bosque Redondo for their own country. Hundreds of Navajos remained confined at Bosque Redondo, but starvation forced them to escape in droves.

Bowing to public pressure, the 1865–1866 Territorial Legislature passed a memorial urging Carleton's removal, which was sent to President Andrew Johnson. The long night of a "punishing Indian policy" was coming to an end. On September 9, 1866, Carleton was relieved of his duties. The anti-Carleton Santa Fe *New Mexican* editorial exalted at his departure.

In June of 1868 a treaty was signed with the Navajos, and thousands started for their homeland. Hundreds had died, they had been deprived of their freedom by the military, but they had survived as a people. The Diné were home.

Rosa paused in her notes. Japanese Americans would suffer a similar punishment during World War II. And back home, thousands of Mexican workers were being deported to Mexico, breaking up families and destroying the dreams of the young, who wished only to finish their education. Did history teach any lessons? Maybe history was no longer being read in the halls of Congress or in the office of a rogue president.

Did the people of the Pecos River know this tragic part of their history? And what could they do when people were punished by an unjust government? Could the young be enticed to read history so they did not make such tragic mistakes in the future?

In our own time, the Muslims will be next if the crazy president has his way. He hates women and all ethnic groups.

"I am becoming a recorder of history," Rosa wrote Marcy.

"That's your mission," came her reply.

"But others have already written about this time and place," Rosa argued.

"Not from your perspective," she replied. "You are now part of that history."

"I can't be!" Rosa protested. "I belong in the future!"

"The past creates the future," came Marcy's reply. "You do have an option: move to Canada, as many are doing. Be safe there to tell the world what is happening with C-Force. Leave everything behind."

"I am here searching for the true history. Is that all I can do?" She closed her laptop with a bang and whispered a silent curse.

19

"You were sitting in the truck when you saw me board the spaceship. What you call a UFO."

Rosa hesitated, then typed in, "I saw something."

"You're not sure?"

"Damn you, Marcy! What am I supposed to say? That a UFO landed and picked you up? I saw something! I thought I saw . . . I was tired . . . ChupaCabra was chasing me . . ."

"You doubt?"

"Yes, I doubt! I've been trained to doubt! I'm supposed to use critical thinking! Let the marvelous real occur in literature, but not in reality!"

Marcy laughed. "Oooo, brujería. What reality? Haven't you been in Billy's world long enough to know you create your own reality?"

"I didn't create this! I came through the wormhole! I didn't know what I was getting into! I want to go home!" She felt like deleting everything. Sometimes communicating with Marcy got to be too much.

"You tangled with ChupaCabra aboard the cruise ship and right in your own backyard. Then in Roswell. Now it's Saytir, and many are depending on you. What you write, people will believe."

"I don't want readers to depend on me." The minute she wrote that, she realized her mistake. Readers did depend on the written word, they always had, ever since the first caveman had scratched his story on a cave wall. This is what I did today, the hunter wrote, and with carbon from the fire he wrote his story on the wall. I went hunting. I killed a deer. My name is Deer Slayer.

"This is what I did. I wrote *The True Story of Billy the Kid*. My name is Rosa Medina. I am related to Deer Slayer."

"Yes, yes," Marcy wrote. "Now you're with it. Your story can destroy Saytir. Find someplace to bury the flash drive so it won't be found. C-Force is more dangerous than ever. The SETI Optical Radio Telescope searches the galaxy for signs of extraterrestrial intelligence. It has received radio signals. Don't you get it? We are the intelligent life in the galaxy, and C-Force wants to capture our brethren to continue its experiments."

"What?"

"SETI received a message. Unfortunately, C-Force has infiltrated SETI. It wants to be there first when our brethren, our neighbors, visit Earth. Their radio signals tell us they have an advanced technology, and they have figured out how *not* to destroy themselves with it."

Rosa was intrigued. "What does this have to do with me?"

"For starters, we know that most advanced technological civilizations destroy themselves in their infancy. Nations create weapons, and once each country has its nuclear arsenal, political forces keep adding to the stockpile. No one wants to disarm. When we acquired nuclear weapons, we fit the rule. You only have to look at the proliferation that's taking place, loose nukes being sold to terrorists. A crazy president with his finger on the nuclear button."

"Nuclear war?"

"Yes. And C-Force doesn't want us to communicate with the vecinos because they can teach us how not to destroy ourselves."

"They're here to help?"

"Yes. Help us by teaching us how to control our urge to bomb ourselves to smithereens. We are a very young civilization, we have outpaced our moral capacity. Sooner rather than later, our deranged president will set off a nuclear bomb. Playing the big macho role. C-Force haunts the halls of the West Wing."

"Saytir in the White House?"

"Now you're on to something. If he pushes the button, the last world war will commence. The end of Earth as we know it. Complete chaos. That's what they want, a dying chaotic world without an ounce of morality. Saytir will rule in chaos."

"Impossible!"

"Oh, yes, even the most chaotic structures operate by internal laws. Saytir wants to be there when the first spaceship lands, and take our brethren prisoners. Concentration camps are already being planned. First the Muslims were rounded up, then refugees, then the Mexicans, then us. Slave camps for experimentation."

"Thanks for the wonderful news. What am I supposed to do?"

"Write Billy's history. Let people know we have this self-destructive instinct in us. It's what led to the violent times in Lincoln. But there was some good in Billy. If you can find some goodness in Billy's life, that's the lesson to be learned and taught to the young. Otherwise we're lost. Your story can save the world."

"I didn't set out to save the world!"

"Few writers do, and yet that's your mission. Your story should tell us that we can destroy ourselves."

Marcy's communication began to fade.

"Are you there? Are you there? Answer me!"

Had Marcy gone crazy? How would comparing Billy's time to our own save the world? Can I find some goodness in Billy's life? Rosa wondered. Can I find goodness after a murderous civil war, after slavery, after the enslavement and genocide of Native Americans, after all the greed that was the cause of violence in New Mexico?

What if there is no goodness? What if there is no morality? What if Billy himself is doomed to failure, a product of the violent times? The self cannot be different from the whole, can it? Maybe saints can rise above the society in which they live, but Billy is no saint. Neither am I.

Is this what the story's all about? Is this the story I'm supposed to write?

"Rosa." Billy's voice shook her out of her thoughts.

"Oh, you startled me."

"Sorry. When you write in that thing, you always come away a bit sad. Why?"

Writing history can be depressing, Rosa thought. You find things best left hidden. The heroes become men with feet of mud.

"I hear voices."

"What were you writin'?"

"To a friend. She wants to know if there's goodness in the world."

Billy thought a while. "My dear mother believed in goodness. Me? I don' know. I guess a person just does what he's got to do. I accept my situation. I did not choose the hand I got to play. I tol' Governor Wallace everything I know. I stood up in court an' named the Chapman killers. An' what did it get me? District Attorney Rynerson wants to get me for Sheriff Brady's death. I'm sorry I killed Joe Grant. I was walkin' away when he drew on me. I was faster."

Rosa nodded. She knew that Joe Grant was a bully who wanted to make a name for himself by killing Billy. Soon other drifters from the Texas Panhandle would come gunning for him. Whoever killed Billy the Kid would have bragging rights. Fastest gun in the territory, just like in the western movies.

But Billy did not seem overly worried. As the bitter cold of another winter set in, he took Rosa back to Lincoln, where he knew she would be more comfortable with Martín and Josefa. Then he and the boys headed back to Fort Sumner.

It had been a difficult year, and there was little to celebrate that Christmas. But Josefa was determined to make the best of it. With Billy gone, Rosa was on her own for the holiday, so Josefa invited her to join them. She prepared a big pot of posole flavored with red chile, tamales, piles of hot sopapillas, biscochitos, and natillas for desert. Martín came home from the saloon holding a bottle of wine. "We celebrate!" he said, a bit tipsy. "We are familia! ¡Feliz Navidad!" The good spirits of Josefa and Martín were infectious. Rosa joined them in singing Christmas carols.

The day before, a chilling snowstorm had blasted down from the Sierra Blanca, but Martín's and Josefa's home was warm and secure. The people had learned to build with adobe, earthen mud bricks cut out from river clay. Yes, the cold air whistled through the door and window cracks, but Josefa stuffed old rags into the cracks and kept out the drafts. They ate, told stories, and sang. Josefa knew many songs, and she led them in singing "Las Mañanitas" to celebrate the birth of Jesus.

> Estas son las mañanitas
> que cantaba el Rey David.
> Hoy por ser día de tu santo,
> te las cantamos a ti.*

And for the Virgin Mary she sang "Cuando por el oriente."

> Cuando por el oriente
> sale la aurora,
> caminaba la Virgen,
> Nuestra Señora.†

"These are old songs our parents taught us," Josefa said. "Now we teach the young."

At midnight they heard singing outside. "¡Los Pastores!" Josefa cried. "The vecinos are singing!" She opened the door, and they stepped out into the cold night to greet some of their neighbors carrying torches. The neighbors had organized a pastorela, the story of the shepherds who traveled to the birth of Jesus. One man carried a sheep on his shoulders. They had stopped to sing "Vamos todos a Belén": Let us go to Bethlehem.

"Oye, Josefa," a man shouted. "¡Vamos a Belén!"

"¡Vamos!" Josefa replied, leading them all in the song.

---

*These are the morning songs
 King David sang.
 Today, the day of your patron saint,
 We sing these songs to you.

†When the light of dawn
 blooms in the east,
 there walks the Virgin Mary,
 our Mother.

Vamos todos a Belén,
con amor y gozo,
adoremos al Señor,
nuestro Redentor.
La noche fue día,
un angel bajó,
nadando entre luces,
que así nos habló.‡

They sang the old verses of the song, and at the end everyone cheered and called out "¡Feliz Navidad!"

"¡Vamos!" the chorus leader called. "Let's go to Juan Patrón's house! He always has candy for the children. ¡Vamos todos a Belén!"

Rosa, Josefa, and Martín joined the chorus making their way to the Patrón home, their path lit by torches, the children shouting in joy, the dogs barking. In the corral, Mancita whinnied.

"This is it!" Rosa exclaimed. "What I've been looking for!"

La Pastorela, a traditional nativity play, has been reenacted for generations in New Mexico. Neighbors gather to sing on Christmas Eve, playing the roles of shepherds making their way to the birth of Jesus.

"The goodness in the people," Rosa whispered as they went down the road singing.

Overhead, the Milky Way and the winter moon were guiding lights. Rosa was sorry she hadn't been able to share this experience with Billy. He loved to sing, and he would have reveled in the joyous celebration that night. As she stood beneath the starry sky, she

---

‡Let us all go to Bethlehem
 With love and joy,
 To adore Jesus Christ,
 Our Savior.
 Night became day,
 An angel came down,
 Swimming in the glowing sky,
 These words to proclaim.

had no way of knowing that the Arrow of Time had turned against Billy Bonney. Fate, a nebulous god, was stronger than any man's will. Billy was in the hands of Pat Garrett, and it would be several eventful months before she would see him again.

20

Rosa hurried down the dusty street to the Lincoln jail. After being tried in Mesilla for the killing of Sheriff Brady, Billy had been transferred back to Lincoln by Judge Warren Bristol, who had ordered "the said William Bonney, alias Kid, alias William Antrim, to be hanged by the neck until his body be dead."

Rosa climbed the stairs to the room where Billy was being held and knocked on the door. Deputies James Bell and Bob Olinger knew Rosa. They let her in.

"Hey, Billy boy," Olinger snickered. "Your lady friend's here to see you."

Rosa pushed by the obnoxious man. Her heart sank the minute she saw the shackled Billy.

"Oh, Billy," she whispered.

A nervous Billy greeted her. "Rosa, I'm glad to see you. How are you?"

"I'm well," she answered, trying to keep her voice calm. She could not bear to see freedom-loving Billy in handcuffs and leg-irons.

"Sit, Rosa. There's so much I have to tell you. Pat Garrett's sheriff now."

"I know," Rosa said, reaching out to touch his hands inside the cold iron of the handcuffs. On November 2, 1880, the citizens of Lincoln County had elected Garrett their sheriff. "Now what, Billy?"

"Garrett knows I politicked for Kimbrell, but John Chisum an' Joe Lea wanted Pat. What the hell, Pat's a good man. He came up to Fort Sumner in late 1878. He'd been hunting buffalo on the llano, an' rustling on the side. Those days I played cards with Pat, an' he always paid his debts."

"But Chisum and Lea wanted you out of the way. So does Mr. Wild from the U.S. Secret Service. You've been passing counterfeit notes."

Billy shrugged. "A boy's got to make a livin'. Rustlin' up in the Texas Panhandle an' drivin' cattle to Los Portales, then to the mines at White Oaks, that's a lot of work. Counterfeit bills are easy."

"You don't have friends at White Oaks."

"Ah, people are fickle. They complain about us, but those miners are happy to eat the beef I sell 'em."

"And Carlyle? The newspapers are accusing you of killing Carlyle at the Greathouse Ranch."

"Here's what happened. The posse jumped us at Coyote Springs. We made our way to the ranch, where the posse pinned us down. Deputy Hudgens sent Carlyle in to parley with us. He an' the boys got to drinkin'. After a few hours, he got in a panic an' jumped out the window. Everyone opened fire, us and his own men outside. So who gets the blame? Billy Bonney. The *Las Vegas Gazette* branded me an outlaw."

"Billy—." Rosa tried to calm him.

"I kilt two men, Joe Grant an' Windy Cahill, I admit. But the papers writ I kilt twenty-one! Not right. Me an' Jesse Evans had a shootout with a group of Mescaleros over some horses. Maybe we left a couple dead, but we was runnin' from them. Grant an' Cahill were bullies, an' both had the drop on me. It was me or them. The other men I get blamed for killin', they died in a gunfight with everyone's bullets flyin'. But I get the blame!"

He took a deep breath, then went on. "I was at the post office, an' folks was readin' a copy of the December 1880 *New York Sun*. Even in the East they call me an outlaw. Wallace has turned tail. Two years ago he promised a pardon an' he reneged. I wrote him an' explained I've been in Fort Sumner makin' my living gamblin', helpin' Abrana with her girls. The rest are plain lies put out by Chisum an' his tools. Wallace placed a five-hundred-dollar reward on my head. The sumbitch was never to be trusted. Neither is Pat Garrett. I knew he'd come huntin' for the reward money."

"So much has happened in a year," Rosa whispered.

"Garrett had spies reportin' to him. When we rode into Fort

Sumner—Wilson, Bowdre, Pickett, Rudabaugh, O'Folliard, and myself—Garrett an' his posse was waitin' in the old hospital building. Tom an' Pickett rode in first, an' Garrett opened fire. Killed Tom; Pickett escaped. We got out of there an' holed up in an old rock house near Stinking Springs. A snowstorm had come down like a hungry wolf. Lord, it was cold.

"But bein' holed up at Stinking Springs warn't so bad. We played cards, did some target practice, roped a couple of mustangs on the llano an' broke them. Mexicanos round there brought us sheep, so we ate like kings. We rustled a few steers, took them into town, and sold them to Pete Maxwell. Weekends we slipped into Fort Sumner an' played cards at Beaver Smith's saloon. I got to see my ladies. I worried about you, but I knew Martín and Josefa would take good care of you."

Rosa listened intently to Billy. She could tell that in his mind he was living those experiences again.

"Then Garrett and his posse tracked us down. Or someone in Fort Sumner told him where we was hidin'. Two days before Christmas I walk out the door, an' there's Garrett an' his posse. Had the place surrounded. He called my name. Bowdre heard him an' came runnin' out. They killed him in cold blood. Never had a chance. We had no chance. They shackled us an' took me, Pickett, Rudabaugh, an' Wilson into Fort Sumner. Manuela Bowdre was crazy with grief. Garrett din't let me see Abrana.

"The day after Christmas, they took us to Las Vegas. The good people cheered for me. Sheriff Romero wanted Garrett to hand over Rudabaugh, but Garrett held his ground. Took us to the railway depot over in New Town an' on to Santa Fe. Garrett turned us over to federal authorities an' collected his five hundred. On New Year's Day, I wrote Governor Wallace from jail. Wrote him again in March. Two years ago he had promised me a pardon for testifyin'. He knew I was bein' sent to Mesilla, an' Judge Bristol was goin' to nail me. Wallace double-crossed me."

"People say he was too busy writing that novel *Ben Hur*."

Billy forced a nervous laugh. "Maybe that's why I don' trust the written word. Most written about me is lies. You tell 'em the truth, Rosa."

Billy could not look into the future. Many books had already been written about him. Lies and truths. Each reader had to come to his or her own conclusion about where the truth lay.

Rosa nodded. "I'll try, Billy."

"So they got me on a federal indictment. Courthouse was a rundown old adobe in the Mesilla plaza. Lookin' at the beautiful old church in the plaza was my only solace. Judge Bristol dismissed the federal charges, but he gets his revenge by turnin' me over to the territorial authorities. He wants to nail me for Sheriff Brady's death. Bonifacio Baca, Billy Mathews, an' Isaac Ellis testified against me. The jury believed Mathews." Billy's voice grew subdued.

After transferring Billy from Mesilla to Lincoln, they had placed him in the upstairs room of the old Murphy-Dolan store, which was serving as the county courthouse. He still expected Wallace to keep his word, but Wallace had told a Las Vegas reporter, "I can't see how a fellow like him should expect any clemency from me."

Rosa grew despondent. Of more than fifty men indicted for offenses during the Lincoln County War, Billy was the only one sentenced to pay with his life. Had justice been served? How would she write the story? No matter which way one read the life of Billy the Kid, there would be those who branded him a killer and those who were sympathetic to him.

"I'm sorry I let you down, Rosa." He glanced around the room, then at his shackles. "I was supposed to protect you. Now look at me, in leg-irons."

"Don't worry about me, Billy. Josefa and Martín take good care of me. They're like parents—" Her voice choked.

"You're in kind of a bind, aren't you? Bein' here."

Rosa nodded. Yes, she had come all this way with Billy, and now he was headed to his fateful day, a meeting with destiny. She wondered if she would ever get back to her room in Puerto de Luna where she had been sitting at her desk the night Billy knocked on the door.

"Josefa said she was going to bring you your favorite meal."

"Josefa is my madrecita. She and Martín have helped me since the day I rode into Lincoln County. I hope I haven't let 'em down."

"It was what you had to do, Billy," was all Rosa could say.

"I'll get out of here. You watch."

"Time's up, lady!" Olinger shouted as he and Bell entered the room.

"Got to go," Rosa said. "I'll come back." She leaned down and kissed him lightly on his lips.

"Glory be," he said, smiling. "First time you ever kissed me."

"Yes," Rosa whispered. Warm tears ran down her cheeks. She wasn't supposed to interfere in his life, and now that one kiss had unburdened the emotions she had felt the past three years. She loved Billy.

"You done, pretty lady?" Olinger sneered. Rosa knew he hit and kicked Billy when Garrett was gone. Shackled, Billy could do nothing. Bell, on the other hand, was kinder. "He is considerate," Billy had told her.

"Be careful," Billy said. Then, to show he wasn't afraid of Olinger, he looked the deputy in the eyes and sang.

> Yo soy el muchacho alegre.
> Si quieren saber quien soy
> pregúntenselo a Cupido.
> Yo soy el muchacho alegre del cielo favorecido.*

Deputy Bell pulled Rosa toward the door just as Olinger raised his rifle and struck Billy across the face. "How's that, pretty boy!"

"No!" Rosa protested, but Bell pushed her out the door. Cursing the deputy, a distraught Rosa went down the stairs and into Lincoln's dusty main street. She shaded her eyes and stared at the shadow in front of her. Saytir.

---

*I am a happy young fellow
 If you want to know who I am
 ask Cupid.
 I am a happy young fellow favored by heaven.

21

Rosa jerked to a stop. Just moments ago she had been consumed with rage over what she had just witnessed, worrying about Billy's plight. Now all that was washed away. Saytir stood in front of her.

She squinted. His costume nearly made her laugh. She knew Coyote the Trickster sometimes dressed in outlandish cowboy outfits, but Saytir's took the cake. Not even the city dudes in the movie *Blazing Saddles* had looked this out of place. Saytir wore purple bell-bottom pants with silver rosettes sewed down the sides of the legs, a bright red shirt, and a dazzling blue satin vest. His neckerchief was pink, his hat a poor excuse for a large mariachi sombrero. His boots were obviously from a Juárez mercado. On his gun belt he sported two silver pistols, one on each hip.

"Rosa," he whispered in his best imitation of Gary Cooper in the movie *High Noon*. "We meet again."

"You!" Rosa cried out, her survival instinct taking over. Should she run or reach for the derringer in her pocket?

"Draw!" Saytir threatened. His reptilian eyes glowed with fire; his hands rested lightly on his pistols.

"You're crazy," Rosa whispered, glancing up and down the street. Not a soul in sight. Not even Pat Garrett. And Josefa's house was a few hundred yards away.

The music from *The Good, the Bad and the Ugly* played in the background. The thin, rattling sound of a rattlesnake about to strike whispered in the summer air. A tumbleweed rolling down the street raised a puff of dust. The clock on the county courthouse wall read high noon. Someone had forgotten to wind it.

When the moment could bear no more tension, Saytir smiled and said, "High noon, Rosa, just like the movie. But I wouldn't kill an unarmed woman. I respect the Law of the West."

Rosa relaxed. Saytir was playing games. He liked costumes. First the sheriff, then the priest, now the outlandish cowboy. He had come for the flash drive.

"How do you like my outfit? We're in the wild west of Lincoln County, so I dressed the part."

"You obviously never rode a horse in your life," Rosa replied. When faced with danger, act as crafty as Odysseus. Confuse the enemy.

Saytir sneered. "Don't act smart. I'm not one of your phony cowboys. I am ChupaCabra!"

I won't forget that, thought Rosa. Saytir was a dangerous and powerful killer. Why was he playing games?

"Where are your sidekicks?"

"Sidekicks? Oh, my fellow Himits? The mavericks I call them. I could only get one through the wormhole, and as you know, Patas Grandes destroyed him. But I'm here."

"For the flash drive."

"Yes."

"How did you get here?" she asked, stalling for time.

"I followed you and Billy through the wormhole. From Puerto de Luna to Lincoln. You and Billy beat me here. From one time dimension to another. If you can travel faster than light, you can travel back in time. Dark energy rules the universe." He laughed, something rattling in his throat. Rosa looked at his eyes. He looked tired. Was he winding down?

"Marcy said some kind of vibration in the galaxy created the wormhole. Cosmic strings woke up the dead, or an exploding supernova."

"Nonsense. What does Marcy know? When a giant star explodes, it creates waves that disturb gravity. That's how wormholes are born. But you're right, there was a vibration. Caused by C-Force."

"What?"

"Yes ma'am. We have an electromagnetic machine big enough and strong enough to warp gravity. A collider of sorts. We have achieved mastery over the biggest riddle in physics: warping space-time."

Rosa knew she needed time, time for Billy to come riding in just like in the movies and rescue her. But he was in jail, shackled in handcuffs and leg-irons. She had to stall.

"I read about the Hadron Collider. They want to find the original particle that binds the universe. Is that what you're getting at?"

"No, we have our own machine. Enough science—the flash drive."

"You're in a hurry. You look tired."

"Nonsense. Just in a hurry for you to give me what I came for. I need to get back to the wormhole."

"You can't create wormholes! No way a machine is big enough to make waves in gravity."

"We can!" Saytir angrily boasted. "Been in the works for years."

"But nothing can travel faster than the speed of light," Rosa protested. "I know that much. According to relativity—"

"Oh, so you've been reading Carl Sagan. Or the Hawking boy. Or the science magazines I found in your study. That's elementary stuff for the masses. Classical laws were superseded by quantum mechanics based on the uncertainty principle. With our machine we can dominate the Arrow of Time—"

What is he getting at? thought Rosa. She had fallen into the past, that much she knew. Or was it only a long, carefully crafted dream? Or another Billy the Kid movie? She had been writing Billy's story, his plot line, and she had fallen into the story. Did Saytir have her over a barrel? Had C-Force truly created a wormhole? Everything was possible in a universe that was giving up its miraculous laws to those who looked into its secrets.

"You can't control the Arrow of Time," she muttered.

"It's elementary, Rosa," Saytir taunted. "You're a beginner, still thinking of time as measured by the clock, where time moves only forward. Did you know there are three Arrows of Time? There's the thermodynamic arrow, or the direction of time in which disorder increases. And we know everything falls from order to disorder sooner or later. The common people call it Murphy's law. Then there's the psychological arrow, in which you humans feel that time passes because you remember the past but cannot see the future. And there's the cosmological Arrow of Time, the direction of time in which the universe is expanding and not contracting. You are a creature of time, Rosa."

"And you were created in a lab by a 3D printer."

"What nonsense," Saytir replied. "I come from a family of ChupaCabras from the mountains of Puerto Rico. I am infused with extraterrestrial DNA. What an achievement! Super ChupaCabra!"

"You were in LA."

"What? Yes, I was feeding dope to barrio kids. Cops said I punctured their skulls with my fangs and sucked out their brains. Nonsense! Meth is what killed their brains! Crack houses, heroin, opioids, and all the other drugs. An epidemic!"

"What is it you really want?"

"Control over the whole enchilada!"

He laughed so hard his pistol belt slipped down to his boots, almost dropping his pants. "Darn!" he cursed, and pulled them back to his hips.

"Why here? Why in Billy's time?"

Saytir shrugged. "Accident. The C-Force machine is new. Some wormholes are difficult to control. I think it was your own doing. You were writing a book about Billy and you got too deep. Just like in a dream."

"Dreams don't have plot lines."

"Suit yourself. It's hot and I have to return . . . before the wormhole closes."

"What do you mean?"

"The wormholes created by the C-Force machine are virtual. Sooner or later they collapse. I have to get back . . ." His voice trailed.

So the wormhole will close, thought Rosa. It's *manmade*, not made in nature. Saytir has to get back before it collapses, but so do I! Billy and I came through the same wormhole. If it closes, I have no other way to get back. Will I stay and ride with Billy for eternity?

"Why the flash drive?" Rosa asked, stalling.

"Your friend Marcy hacked the C-Force computers and took everything. Even the cloud data. The flash drive is all we have. It contains the genome formulas of the extraterrestrial and ChupaCabra. Ipso facto, you have me! ChupaCabra! Bloodsucker! Shapeshifter! Terminator! Dopester! C-Borg! Yes, we feed dope to the young so we can control them! How do you like that! With time we can reconstruct the genome—"

"But there isn't time, is there?"

"Time! Time! Time!" Saytir exploded, then cringed as if an electrical spasm had contracted his body. "I don't have time!" he shouted. "I need the alien DNA!"

It dawned on Rosa that Saytir was losing whatever energy the alien DNA had provided. He needed a fix!

"You're sick," she whispered, words Saytir felt like the strike of a rattlesnake.

"I need the flash drive! I don't need C-Force or the crazy president! I can go my own way! I am Destroyer of Worlds!" He was mumbling, becoming wavelengths of light before her eyes.

"If you kill me, you'll never find it."

"Damn you, Rosa! All of this has been a terrible mistake. I need to get back. The wormhole *will* close. I haven't time—" He gritted his teeth, exhaling a yellowish mist.

Ah, thought Rosa, Saytir and his Himits think they can control the Arrow of Time, but they can't.

"You're dying."

"I'm invincible! I won't die!"

"Then you're passing from *order*, the form C-Force gave you, into *disorder*. Entropy. You haven't learned to reverse the second law of thermodynamics! Complete disorder means your antiparticles will scatter in the galaxy—"

"No!" Saytir cried. "You don't know what you're talking about!"

"I think I do," Rosa said, taunting him. "Shapeshifter. The witches, Yenadlooshi, my Uncle José called them. He told me how they could change into animal forms. Every culture has such stories. The Aztecs, the Vikings, the medieval Catholic Church. Now you! A technological monster, but the technology is not foolproof. That's why Nadine and Billy were able to kill Himits, and why Patas Grandes could destroy the last one. You're vulnerable!"

"You think you're so damn smart!" Saytir blasted, his breath creating the similitude of a black hole where a giant star has just collapsed, a black hole so big that the contracting universe would eventually collapse into it. Not even light could escape from a black hole. Once past the event horizon, even dust particles were gobbled up.

"You're dying. Creating your own destruction!"

"I'm invincible! Better than John Wayne! More infallible than the pope!"

The empty space of the street suddenly filled with pairs of virtual particles and antiparticles. Was Saytir exhausting his laboratory life?

"Give me what I came for!" he roared. "And I will allow you to return to the future. Return home. Otherwise you will be trapped here forever!"

Rosa trembled. Trapped in the past, repeating it without being able to affect it. A hell worse than Dante's Inferno.

At that moment, the door of the courthouse opened, and Deputy Bob Olinger marched out with five prisoners, escorting them across the street for an early supper at the Wortley Hotel.

Olinger did not know he had only minutes left to live.

22

Upstairs, Billy had finished an early supper of ham, grits, tortillas, and coffee. He stood and asked Deputy Bell if he could use the privy behind the courthouse. Bell nodded, checked Billy's cuffs and leg-irons, then led him downstairs to the outhouse in back.

The rattlesnake coiled in Billy's brain had more in mind than the use of the privy. Olinger was gone, and Billy knew that if he didn't make a move now, the circumstances might not present themselves again.

On the way back, Billy, although in leg-irons and handcuffs, hurried up the stairs and turned into the hall. He had practiced slipping the cuff off one wrist, which he did now. When Bell appeared, Billy swung the chain, and the cuff caught Bell full in the face. "Damn you, Billy!" Bell cried as he went down.

Billy jumped him. The two wrestled for Bell's pistol, and Billy wrenched it away. "Sorry, Bell, but I don' aim to swing!"

"An' I don't aim to die!" Bell exclaimed, and started for the stairs.

Still on the floor, Billy fired. Critically shot, Bell stumbled down the stairs, out the back door, and into the arms of Godfrey Gauss, who was walking by. Old Gauss knew that Billy was being held prisoner upstairs, and he guessed what had happened. "Lord save you," he whispered, and laid the dead man on the ground.

"I din't want to kill him!" Billy shouted to Gauss. "But I have to save my own life." He shuffled into Garrett's office, picked up Olinger's shotgun, and made his way to the porch. He knew Olinger would hear the shot and come running.

A frightened Gauss shouted to Olinger, "The Kid killed Bell! The Kid killed Bell!" Hearing the gunshot and the shouting, several citizens appeared in the street.

Olinger, too, had heard the gunshot. He hurried across the street and opened the wood gate in front of the courthouse. Looking up, he stared straight into the shotgun Billy was pointing at him. "I'm dead!" he cried, going for his pistol, realizing he had walked into a trap.

"You won't bully me no more!" Billy shouted. He let go with both barrels. The heavy buckshot caught Olinger full on the chest and spun him back into the street, where he fell dead.

Billy hurried to a south window and called to Gauss, "I got to break these chains. There's a pickaxe sitting by the privy. Throw it up here." Gauss had been a cook at Tunstall's Río Feliz rancho years earlier, where he had gotten to know Billy. Acting out of both friendship and fear, he grabbed the pickaxe and heaved it up. "Up it goes!" Billy took the pick, sat down, and hammered at the chain attached to the leg shackles. Sparks flew, and after a few whacks the chain was severed, giving him added movement.

By now a group of men, including the five prisoners, had gathered around Olinger, who lay dead on the street. According to Gauss, Bell was also dead.

"What the hell do we do?" a man asked.

"I aim to get my rifle," one answered, but others held him back.

"You crazy. That's the Kid up there."

That was warning enough to dissuade him. Nobody was brave or foolish enough to take on Billy. Besides, half the town would side with Billy in a gun battle. Best to let things play out, and they didn't have long to wait.

"There he is!"

"¡Bilito!" a vaquero shouted. "¿Qué pasó?"

"¡Maté a ese cabrón!" Billy spat down from the porch. He smashed Olinger's shotgun on the porch railing and threw the pieces down at the bloody corpse. "Here's your gun, you damned fool! You won't be stickin' it in my ribs any longer!"

He paused and looked down at the gathered crowd. He was sweating and breathing hard. He had just killed two men, and the impact of the deed rattled him. For a few moments he stood staring at the frightened citizens. "I'm sorry I killed Bell," he said to the crowd. "I grabbed his revolver an' tol' him not to run. I would have tied him up an' let him be. But he ran, an' it was either him or me."

He paused again, and his voice rose. "Olinger was a bully. I had no use for him. Always proddin' me with his shotgun. Well, he got it back. We're even. As for the rest of you, don' anyone come toward me. I mean to escape. I'm armed an' I don' mean to swing. I need no more innocent lives on my conscience."

He bowed his head as if in prayer. Then he called down, "I am innocent! I know I killed, but that's the law of the territory, the law of Lincoln County. A man has to protect hisself. We don' carry guns for purty, we carry them for protection. Maybe we shouldn't, but that's the way it is."

He looked into the late afternoon sun, with its summer brilliancy lighting up spring clouds that had moved in. Within the hour it would set over Sierra Blanca. The valleys would go dark with gloom. The night would be long for those who would stay up late telling and retelling the story of the day.

History was being written for the instant, but the Arrow of Time would move on. Those who lived through that April afternoon were witness to only part of what had come and what was to come. Not a man alive could have prophesized how the story would end.

Again Billy spoke. "I got caught up in these events because the Dolan/Murphy gang killed Mr. Tunstall. He was a fair an' decent man. Treated me like a son. I set out to avenge his death. Maybe that's not right, but I did. Revenge is the law of this country as it is the law of the jungle. My good mother taught me a story writ by Shakespeare. Anthony would avenge the death of Caesar. 'Never take the law into your own hands,' she warned me. 'Without law there is no civilization . . .'"

He twisted as if in pain, then looked away. Catching his breath, he continued. "I done her wrong. Today I sealed my fate. The law will have its vengeance. But I ask you this: Why in all the killin' an' thievin' that's gone on am I the only one convicted to die? All of you know the story of the Lincoln County War. Don' pretend innocence.

Be witness to the events that happened here, as you are witness in church."

He paused.

A village dog missing one of its front paws limped up to sniff at the dead man. Two other mongrels held back, nervous, whining. A vaquero standing nearby shooed them, and the dogs went cringing away. The dogs in Lincoln were used to dead men lying in the street. Poor dog, handicapped like me, thought Billy. He looked down at his leg-irons and chain. I din't have a dog when I was a kid. No father. Had a stepfather for a while. Mother died an' left me an orphan. I had to learn to protect myself from the bullies, so I took up the gun. The territory is a violent place.

"Gauss!" he shouted. "Burt's horse is in the corral out back. Saddle it up. I aim to ride." Gauss ran to do as he was told and shortly brought the horse out front. Billy descended, carrying an armful of pistols and rifles. He stopped at Olinger's body and nudged the corpse with his boot. "You will never round me up again, damn you. Never whip another man in chains."

He started to mount, but armed as he was, the skittish horse reared up and ran. Billy called out, "Alex, get that pony an' bring it!" The man hesitated, but he quickly ran after the horse when Billy pointed a pistol. He brought it over and held it while Billy mounted. With that brief deed, Alex Nunnelly would enter the history books.

Billy called to Rosa. "Rosa! Let's ride!"

"Damn!" Saytir cursed. "He's broken out of jail! Time for me to move on."

"What happened?" Rosa asked, rubbing her eyes. The Himit standing in front of her was no longer the ridiculous cowboy she had been arguing with, but a metallic ChupaCabra, its eyes burning with fire. Saytir as Terminator.

"Hypnosis, Rosa. You know I like to play games. Thought this way I could get the flash drive from you without tangling with Billy."

"He has power over you, doesn't he? In his time you can't harm him."

"Nonsense!" Saytir shouted. "C-Force creates time!"

"Rosa!" Billy called again. He was standing in the street surrounded by townspeople.

"The story's not over," Saytir hissed. "See you in D.C." He backed into the shade of a building, spread his bat wings, and disappeared.

"¡Aquí, Rosa!" someone called. Martín and Josefa came up, he leading Mancita. "Tu cajita in saddlebag. Here tu backpack," Josefa said. "Comida, some apples."

"Gracias," Rosa replied. "Tu cajita" meant her laptop. She was ready to leave Lincoln.

Martín tied the saddlebag and the backpack to the saddle. "You ready," he said and hugged her.

"Adiós, Rosa. ¡Que vayas con Dios!" Josefa kissed and blessed her. She waved at the waiting Billy. "¡Adiós, Bilito! ¡Cuídate!"

Martín helped Rosa mount. She pressed her legs into the mare's sides and the horse jumped forward, following Billy out of town, leaving a cloud of dust rising in the last light of day.

23

They rode east into the darkening plain, the Llano Estacado of so much promise, so much bloodshed, leaving behind a shocked Lincoln citizenry burying their dead.

The next day, April 29, 1881, in White Oaks, Pat Garrett heard about the escape. He cursed the Kid, his deputies, and himself. "I told 'em the Kid will not stay put. Do not let your guard down. I shoulda been there. He has too many friends in town. Los Mexicanos are his amigos. They watch out for him." Garrett quickly telegrammed Governor Wallace. "I have just received news from Lincoln . . . that Billy the Kid escaped yesterday . . . after killing Deputy Sheriffs J. W. Bell and Bob Olinger. I cain't hang a man who's not my prisoner."

Billy and Rosa rode into the Capitán foothills to the home of Ataviano Salas. He did not have the tools to cut through the leg-irons, so they rode on to José Córdova's ranch in Salazar Canyon, where Billy's old acquaintances Córdova and Scipio Salazar freed him from the shackles. "Go to Mexico," Salazar suggested while they ate. "Here you have too much money on your head."

"I got a score to settle," Billy replied.

Forget the score, Rosa thought. Take your friends' advice and head south. You can't, can you? That's not the way your story ends, not in a friendly village in Mexico with a wife, raising a family, planting corn, playing cards with the campesinos, enjoying Saturday night dances.

The thought brought tears to her eyes, but she said nothing. So much silence wrapped around the brief young life of el Bilito. Beloved by some and hated by others. She wondered if silence was an integral part of space-time. Silence was the gravity Newton discovered in the falling apple.

They spent a few days with friends, then rode on to Yginio Salazar's place in Las Tablas. "¡Compadre!" Yginio greeted Billy. The Lincoln County War had made them compadres, a friendship formed under fire. Again the advice was the same: "Go to Mexico, Bilito. Ese Garrett Patas Largas is lookin' for you. You know he want the reward."

Again Billy shook his head. After a three-day stay, they rode on to the Peñasco and John Meadows's cabin. Meadows suspected that Billy had come to settle a score with Billy Mathews. "You come for Mathews?" he asked.

"I changed my mind," Billy replied. "He ain't worth killin'."

"Head for old Mexico, Billy. You know the people. You'll be safe there. Here they're gonna come after you. Garrett aims to gun you down. Or you'll get him. Either way it's no good."

Billy looked at Rosa, who, as was her custom, remained quiet. She could write the history of the time she had fallen into, but she could not influence it. Saytir's wormhole, if that's what had got her into this dream, allowed travel into the past, but there was a formidable rule that applied to time travel: You could not kill your grandfather in past time.

Deep in her heart, she knew that Billy would head for Fort Sumner. The people there would protect him as much as they could. Abrana was there.

And that is why, as their time together drew to a close, they rode north to Fort Sumner in the harsh light of May, when the llano grass is greening and hardy flowers dot the landscape. North along the Pecos River, the divine river that deserved the writing of its own history. Magical river of la gente. River of Puerto de Luna apples, corn, calabacitas, the best chile in New Mexico. River of owls and hawks, coyotes and snakes, its chocolate waters a kingdom for catfish and carp, river of curanderas, women worn to the bone with backbreaking work, vaqueros hard as the barbed wire they began to despise.

Cuando llegó el alambre, llegó el hambre. But they went on fencing the land because the open range and land-grant common lands were disappearing.

"I love this river," Billy whispered, standing on the bank, the water roiling south to marry the Río Grande and honeymoon on to the sea.

The river was his life, as was the llano and every living creature on it. Overhead, a bank of cotton-candy clouds descended on the land, the sun's rainbow colors caught in the fluff.

In Fort Sumner, Rosa found safe haven with Abrana García, and the history she recorded on her laptop would reveal many secrets if she could get them back home. After all, it was a detailed history not just of Abrana, but of all the women who lived in this windswept land that boiled in summer and froze in winter. Women who worked from daybreak to late in the night, raising their families, caring for the sick, burying the dead. They kept small, meaningful items tucked in trasteros, marriage licenses if those were to be had, birth certificates when a doctor had been present to sign one, a letter from a son who had moved to California, and a statue of the Virgin Mary bought from a Mexican vendor who had passed by. All these small things reminded them that no matter how hard life was, they kept a smidgen of civilization alive in that harsh land. Someone wrote: they suffered.

Billy stole a horse belonging to Montgomery Bell and immediately drew the attention of the local law. Deputy Sheriff Barney Mason and Jim Cureton followed his trail out to a sheep camp on the llano. Four heavily armed Mexicano sheepherders stood with Billy.

Facing Billy and the Mexicanos, Mason backed off. He had threatened to shoot Billy at Stinking Springs, and he knew Billy never forgot a threat. "Ah, let him be," Mason cursed. "Every damn Messican hereabouts is gonna side with Billy."

Billy seemed unshaken, carefree. He was welcomed at every sheep camp, where there was always food and a place to sleep. Even some ranchers made him welcome. He slipped in and out of Fort Sumner to visit with Abrana and to enjoy the bailes.

The outside world had taken note of Billy's escape from the Lincoln jail. The New York and San Francisco papers kept the public up to date on the escapades of the fearless Kid. Billy's reputation had gone from local color to international. The *Police Gazette* reported his escape in the most colorful police prose of the time. In June the *New*

Mexican truthfully reported that "the people regard him with a feeling half of fear and half of admiration, submit to his depredation, and some of them even go so far as to aid him in avoiding capture."

Some Anglo ranchers knew Billy well, and they kept quiet when he was around. He had friends from the old Regulator gang, but it was more often the Mexicanos who stood by him. These Hispanos lived the history of the land. They knew well the events that had cast Billy into the role of outlaw.

In an interview with a reporter, Governor Wallace announced that he was putting up another five-hundred-dollar reward for the capture of Billy the Kid. "It is our manifest destiny to Christianize this land," he observed. A reporter reminded him that Hispanos were Christians, and some of the Indian pueblos had also incorporated elements of Christianity into their way of life. "I mean we must bring Anglo-American civilization to the backward Mexicans," Wallace responded. "Without our help they cannot thrive. We must root out desperados like the Kid and those who help him."

With those white nationalist sentiments in mind, Wallace left New Mexico, never to return. He had been appointed minister to the Turkish sultan. *Ben-Hur* tucked between his legs, the man who could have saved Billy fled.

"¿Cómo 'stás, Rosa?"

"Bien," Rosa replied. "¿Y tú?"

"Alright, I guess," Billy replied. "You okay here?"

"Yes. The women are good to me."

"You still writin' in your cajita?"

"Oh, yes. I have the time and all these interesting women, each with her own story. You have a lot of adoring fans."

Billy blushed. "Ah, it's just cause I like to dance."

"You haven't missed one," Rosa teased.

"Life's too short."

"You're twenty-one, Henry McCarty. You've got—"

For a moment neither said anything. A hot wind whipped across the empty plain. Cattle called in the distance. A dog barked. A rattlesnake snapped up a mouse that had come too near. Turkey vultures glided effortlessly in the wide blue sky, looking for death. A red-tailed hawk dove, and suddenly the piercing cry of a jackrabbit was heard: the hawk had struck. Every living creature on the llano was hunting.

"First time you ever called me Henry."

"Is it okay?"

"Yeah, okay. Just that it seems Henry died a long time ago. That boy who rode the railroad with his mother an' brother across the Great Plains to Kansas, Colorado, then Silver City, just disappeared. Mother an' brother Joe gone. I was left alone, William Bonney, el Bilito."

"Time makes something new of us all," Rosa said.

"I guess. You feel safe here?"

"Yes."

"No more of that Saytir character?"

"He spread his bat wings and disappeared the day you broke out of jail."

"He will appear somewhere, that's for sure. Just like the devil appears when you least expect it."

I never believed in the devil, Rosa thought. Not the hairy horned beast that lives in a lake of fire. But I have come to believe in Saytir. The C-Force scientists got way out of hand when they combined alien DNA with ChupaCabra's. Are Himits our new devils, or just creatures of a science gone mad?

"All I know is what Marcy tol' me. I seem to be doin' exactly what I ought to do. I know it's hard on you."

"I've adjusted," Rosa said. "Do you think the wormhole was really closing? And that's why Saytir left?"

Billy chuckled. "The only wormholes I know is in apples. Some of the paisanos have fine orchards. The Río Hondo water makes sweet apples. Josefa dries slices in the sun, an' come winter she bakes the most delicious pies."

"She is a wonderful woman. I feel privileged to have met her and Martín, and all the others."

"They're the salt of the earth. They know I cain't go back an' change things."

"No, you cain't," Rosa agreed.

Billy smiled. "You're in good humor. Anyway, the best wormhole I know is the river. When you're ready, follow the river to Puerto de Luna."

Rosa didn't understand. What did he mean, follow the river? They had come downriver in the wormhole created by Saytir, or so she thought. Suddenly her good humor turned ill. Saytir had said the wormhole was closing. If she wasn't at the mouth of the wormhole before it closed, she might be stuck in Billy's history, repeating it forever, unto one followed by twenty-four zeros: 1,000,000,000,000,000, 000,000,000 years. It wasn't the breeze that made her shiver.

"Don' worry. We will get you back to your home in Puerto de Luna if I have to go with you myself."

He couldn't, thought a depressed Rosa. He couldn't. He had only a couple of months left. He was going to die at the hands of Pat Garrett. Nothing could change that.

Billy was confident. Carefree and confident, not knowing his fateful day loomed just ahead. Sheriff Garrett was gathering deputies to ride to Fort Sumner. Every living creature on the llano was hunting.

24

On July 10, Garrett rode out of Roswell. With him were Deputies John Poe and Tip McKinney.

"The Kid has gall," Garrett said to the deputies. "He lingers around Fort Sumner without a care. Don' he know I aim to come after him?"

"I come down from the Texas Panhandle chasing rustlers," Poe said in his slow southern drawl. "Every damn sheepherder and some ranchers stood by Billy. They love that boy."

"I know. I wrote Manuel Brazil to join us. It's obvious he ain't here."

They stood at Taiban Creek below Fort Sumner looking across the empty llano, rolling cigarettes from a tobacco pouch they passed around. The kerchiefs tied round their necks were wet with sweat.

Beneath the tall yuccas, jackrabbits and cottontails sought refuge from the heat. A July mirage opened up and shimmered, moving across the plain with its empty promise of water, then disappearing.

"Hot."

"Hotter'n hell."

"Yeah."

They rode into Fort Sumner and took cover in the apple orchard on the north side of town. "Go by the cantina, John," Garrett said to his deputy. "Folks here don' know you. But be careful. If the Kid knows you're asking for him, there'll be hell to pay."

Poe made his way to Beaver Smith's saloon and ordered a beer. "Where you be from, stranger?" Beaver asked as he wiped the table.

"I come down from the Panhandle," Poe said, looking in a friendly way at two Mexicanos sitting across the room. "Been running cattle for Chisum. Hear the Kid escaped from the Lincoln jail."

The Mexicanos reached for their Winchesters and glared at Poe, who quickly paid his bill and scurried out. They were not going to give Billy up. He rode up the Pecos to Milnor Rudulph's place, but gathered little information. "No one's talking," he reported back to Garrett.

"They be afraid the Kid might show up," Garrett said. "It's dark enough. Let us move in with caution. Pete Maxwell might know a thing or two."

"What day is it?"

"I reckon the 14th."

Few calendars marked the passing of time on the llano. Seasons told the time. It was either blazing hot, stone cold, or windy. Few of the denizens could pause long enough to consider the consequences of the Arrow of Time. Sunup to sundown there was work to be done by the people of the Pecos Valley. That's all there was, backbreaking work, plus maybe a dance and a few drinks on Saturday night. Neighbors visited and helped each other.

Coal oil lamps lighted the windows of the village. The Fort Sumner people had finished supper, and most were ready for bed. By and large they worked for Pete Maxwell, whose father, Lucien Maxwell, had bought the fort and grounds from the government in 1871. Lucien had sold the large Maxwell Land Grant in northern New Mexico, most of which he had stolen from old Mexican and Spanish land grants. With thirty families from the Taos area, he had moved lock, stock, and barrel to Fort Sumner. His Mexicano peones cared for his sheep and cattle. Now Pete Maxwell ran the place. He was a rico, a man of wealth. "Got to talk to Pete," Garrett whispered, aware the bright moon might give them away.

About that time, Billy and Francisco Lobato rode into town. Lobato had a sheep camp on the llano, and Billy often hid out there. Tonight they headed for the home of a friend, Jesús Silva. They stabled the horses and entered Silva's adobe.

"Jesús, ¿cómo 'stás?"

"¡Bilito! ¡Francisco! Entren, entren."

"Jesús, who are those boys camped in the orchard?" Billy asked.

"No sé," Silva replied. "Maybe vaqueros look for work."

"Hay que tener cuidado," Lobato cautioned.

"Tengo hambre," Billy said. "¿Tienes carne?"

"No tengo," Silva replied. "Only beans and tortillas. But don Pedro killed a beef esta mañana. It hangs on his porch."

Billy removed his vest and boots and picked up a knife. "I'm goin' to get us some steaks. You get that stove hot." He went out whistling.

As fate would have it, Garrett and his two deputies had just arrived at the Maxwell house. Garrett knew that don Pedro, as the workers called him, slept in a southeast corner room of the big house. It being a hot summer night, the door and windows would be open.

Garrett looked across the village. Shadows moved in the night. The moonlight revealed a man on his way to the privy; another, perhaps a young man visiting his querida, knocked on a door and disappeared into the house; down the line, a man entered his home after checking his horse before going to bed. Then all was quiet.

The silence made Garrett nervous. A pack of coyotes called in the hills. He could tell by their cries they had made a kill, a desert rat or a raccoon. And thar be rattlers, he thought, large flat-headed diamond backs that come out at night to hunt. They lie in wait under porches or on the path to the privy. Lord, how many horses have I seen stung by rattlers. Leg puffs up, got to drain the poison right away. Seen a few put down. And sheep and cattle. Seen them bit on the nose. That's worse. If they survive, they go blind. Cain't eat for a week or two. Coyotes take them easy. Food chain. That's how nature works. The weak are devoured.

A squealing sound made him jump. He toppled into Poe. "You okay?" Poe asked. "You're sweating."

"I'm okay," Garrett said and looked down. In the dim light he saw he had stepped on a big river toad. His boot had disemboweled the toad, and still it jumped away, dragging its slimy entrails.

"Damn," Garrett cursed. He wiped his boot with his kerchief. "Wait here," he said to Poe. "I'm gonna see Pete." He went up on the porch and called from the door, "Pete, it's me, Pat Garrett. You awake?"

"I am," Maxwell replied. Garrett entered and walked to the bed.

"I'm looking for the Kid. Is he here?"

"He comes by from time to time to see Abrana," Maxwell replied. In the flickering candlelight he recognized Garrett. The sweat of fear was on him.

"He broke out of the Lincoln jail."

"I heard," Maxwell said. "Kind of late, ain't it?"

"I figure he would head here. Listen! There's someone outside. Snuff the candle."

Billy had just approached the hanging beef when he spied Poe. Startled, he asked. "¿Quién es? ¿Quién es?" Poe didn't recognize Billy, but he knew that coming up on a nervous vaquero in the dark was not good. Whoever it was had the drop on him.

"Amigo," Poe said, holding up his hands. "Está bien—"

"¿Cómo te llamas?" Billy asked.

"Amigo," Poe repeated, not knowing much Spanish. "Amigo. Ya voy." He turned and disappeared.

Billy relaxed. The man had not gone for his pistol. Could be one of the cowboys camped at the orchard. A second one stood just beyond the picket fence.

Something didn't feel right. The night had grown ominous. The crickets had suddenly stopped chirping. A silence hung over the land. Billy heard the long, mournful cry of a woman. La Llorona of the Pecos River. The Mexicanos told stories of the crying woman who haunted the river. In a fit of rage she had drowned her son, and now she spent nights looking for him, crying like a demented soul.

Billy jumped up on the porch and called at Maxwell's door. "Pete, it's me, Billy. Who are those fellows outside?"

A frightened Maxwell recognized Billy's voice. He clutched at Garrett and called out, "That's him!"

"¿Quién es? ¿Quién es?" Billy shouted, spying Garrett crouched beside the bed.

Outlined against the door, Billy was an easy target. Garrett stood, aimed, and fired. The bullet caught Billy in the chest, and he lurched forward. Garrett fired a second shot. "Coward!" Billy cried as he went down. "I had no chance." In a fair fight he could have outdrawn Garrett, but the Arrow of Time did not distinguish between good and bad. Billy's destiny had caught up with him.

"It's Billy!" Garrett cried. He jumped toward the door and out of the room. A terrified Pete Maxwell followed him, and both tumbled onto the porch.

"It's the kid! I got him! I heard him groan!" Garrett shouted.

Poe came up and grabbed hold of Garrett and said, "Put your gun away, Pat! You shot the wrong man! The Kid would never let you get the drop on him. You have shot the wrong man!"

Garrett fell to his knees. "I know his voice. It is him!"

Doors banged open, and men came running. Some held lighted coal oil lanterns, some carried rifles. "¿Qué pasó? ¿Qué pasó?" they called. "Mira, Patricio Garrett!"

Pete Maxwell collected himself, ran to his mother's room, and returned with a lighted candle, which he placed on the windowsill. "Go make sure," he said to Garrett, but a trembling Garrett hesitated.

Poe peered into the dark room. By the candle's light he could see the dead body.

Garrett took a deep breath and whispered, "I have kilt Billy the Kid."

25

Hearing the shots, the women dropped whatever they were doing and went out into the night. Who were they?

Abrana and Rosa.

Deluvina Maxwell, the old Navajo woman who had served the Maxwells for many years.

Celsa Gutiérrez, whose sister was married to Pat Garrett.

Paulita Maxwell, Pete Maxwell's sister.

Nasaria Yerby, Tom Yerby's eighteen-year-old housekeeper, and Manuela, Charlie Bowdre's wife.

A woman's cry split the darkness. Was it Rosa? She had known exactly when Billy would meet his fated end.

It is said that some women have the faculty of knowing when danger has come upon their loved one. Even if the loved one is far away.

Abrana dropped her yarning needles and the ball of yarn. Her face turned pale in the dim light of the lantern. She clutched at her stomach as if in pain and looked at Rosa, who sat at the small table.

For hours Rosa had been writing on her laptop. She had come to the end, the precise moment of Billy's death. "Virgin Mary," she wrote, "please deflect the Arrow of Time. Let Billy live, change the fateful hour." It was not to be. A terrible, heart-rending emotion seized her. The vaquero she had been riding with these past three years had just been killed. She could not have stopped Garrett; she could not change the past.

These women, along with other of the Mexicanas and their men, went running to the Maxwell house. "¿Qué pasó? ¿Qué pasó?" they cried as they lit faroles and candles and went out into the night, the men pulling up their britches and boots and grabbing their rifles.

Pat Garrett and his two deputies stood outside the house, rifles at the ready. Pete Maxwell, his mother, his sister Paulita, and some of his servants had joined Garrett.

"¿Qué pasó?" a man asked.

"Garrett dice que mató a Bilito—"

"¡Válgame Dios!"

All made the sign of the cross. It was not possible. El Bilito could not be dead.

"He came to get meat," Lobato said.

"Go in," Jesús Silva said to Garrett. "Go see."

Garrett shook his head. He didn't want to enter the room. What if the Kid was still alive?

"I go," Deluvina said. She grabbed a lighted candle and went in, followed by Rosa, Abrana, and Jesús Silva.

The old woman knelt by the body, turned it, and saw where the bullets had entered near the heart. When she saw it was Billy she wept, a cry so torn from the depths of her soul that those standing outside made the sign of the cross and gathered closer to each other.

Deluvina loved Billy like a son; her cry meant he was dead.

Abrana also wept. He was the love of her life. Now he was dead.

Rosa, too, cried. She felt like an illusion in a time where she didn't belong, a ghost who had journeyed into the past. Still, she could not keep in check the tears that wet her cheeks.

Deluvina's candle sputtered and died.

Rosa took Abrana by the shoulders and led her outside, where the women gathered around her and consoled her. Deluvina emerged holding the dead candle, the melted wax hardening on her hand. "¡Mi hijito está muerto!" she cried. "My son is dead! Bilito is dead." Spying Garrett in the light of the lanterns, she went up to him and pounded on his chest, crying, "You murdered my son, my Bilito. You sumbiche! In the dark you came like a coward and shot him!" The women pulled her away.

"I am the sheriff of Lincoln County," Garrett shouted. "I have the right to protect myself. Billy shot at me and I returned fire. It was him or me!"

Celsa Gutiérrez also cursed Garrett, as did the men. They shouted threats at the sheriff and his deputies. They were fond of Billy, and lamented that he should be lying dead in Pete Maxwell's room. Shot in the dark. They didn't know if Maxwell had had anything to do with the assassination.

Garrett and his two deputies pulled back, rifles at the ready. "All of you go to your homes," Garrett ordered. "There be nothing to do tonight. This is an order. Go home!"

"Let us take the body," Deluvina cried.

"I cain't," Garrett replied. "I need to do this right. Tomorrow Justice of the Peace Segura must convene a coroner's jury. We cain't move the body."

He looked at the angry faces of the men and at Segura, who nodded. It was as the sheriff said: a coroner's jury would have to sign the report. But now it was past midnight, best to wait till morning.

"Go home," Garrett repeated. "I aim to do this right."

The crowd dissolved slowly. The initial anger had subsided. If they killed Garrett and the deputies, what would that solve? Revenge could not bring Billy back.

Garrett breathed a sigh of relief. Billy's friends were angry. The fear he had felt in Maxwell's room had returned. The thing had not gone right. Why had he shot? Was Billy armed? Of course he was, for the Kid never went unarmed. Still, he had the deputies with him. Could they have taken Billy alive? No, he must never believe that. The Kid had moved in the dark, and that meant he was going for his pistol. That's how he would write the report.

"You okay, Pat?" Poe touched Garrett's shoulder.

"I'm okay," Garrett replied. "Best get some rest. Stand guard. Cain't let them take the body."

Early the following morning, Rosa went with some women to claim Billy's body. A group of angry men had gathered in front of the Maxwell house. Many had stayed up all night. They were armed. One carried a rope. The Mexicanos were ready to lynch Garrett and his deputies, who were hiding in the house.

The situation was tense. The men believed that Garrett had killed el Bilito in a cowardly fashion. Jesús Silva had told them that Billy did not have a pistol, only the knife he had taken to cut the meat. Garrett and his deputies could easily have overpowered him. And why had Pete Maxwell let Garrett enter his room? There were too many unanswered questions.

Someone had gone to Milnor Rudulph's home to tell him the news. When he and his son rode in, Garrett, who had not slept all night, looked relieved. "I have the report here," Garrett said, handing a paper to Rudulph. Garrett had written the jury's report beforehand. He wanted to make sure he collected the reward money.

Justice of the Peace Alejandro Segura also turned to Rudulph. "You pick the jury, Milnor," he said. Rudulph looked at the crowd and picked five men. Rosa did not recognize them, but Abrana told her later they were Lorenzo Jaramillo, José Silva, Antonio Saavedra, Sabal Gutiérrez, and Paco Anaya. Paco would later write an account of the tragic night.

They entered the room where Billy lay. Garrett and Maxwell told what had happened, and Rudulph wrote something to the effect that Garrett's action was justifiable homicide and that the community should be grateful to him, and he deserved the reward money. The jurors could not read, but they signed the report anyway. Later, when they found out they had praised Garrett, they were angry, but it was too late. The deed was done; they had been fooled.

The women then asked for the corpse, and the men carried it to the carpenter shop and laid it on a workbench. They dressed Billy in a twenty-five-dollar suit one of the men offered. Jesús Silva built the coffin. The women placed candles around it and prayed a rosary.

Just before Silva nailed the top on the coffin, Rosa, who had been kneeling next to it, stood and leaned over for one last look at Billy. He looked handsome in the borrowed suit, a peaceful look on his face. What did he know of his fate? Only that one day he would have to meet la muerte. The Arrow of Time had pierced his heart so deep that there had been no time for reflection.

What would he have said? Adiós, mi gente. Thank all of you for taking me into your homes. When I was ragged and hungry, you fed me. When the law came looking for me, you hid me. Thanks to all the fathers who let me dance with their beautiful daughters. Write that on my tombstone.

A sobbing Rosa took the flash drive from her pocket and slipped it into the coffin. It would be buried with Billy, and no one would know. But what if the body was exhumed in the future, as some in her time had talked of doing? Would they find the flash drive?

She said a silent goodbye to the young man she had gotten to know so well and went to sit with the women.

Billy received a proper wake, a custom in keeping with his Irish past. The Mexicanos of the valley had long practiced the velorio for the dead, praying a rosary and singing alabados.

Jesús Silva and Vicente Otero dug the grave in the old military cemetery. The mourners gathered around the gravesite for one last goodbye. "Sing a song for Billy," Jesús asked Paco, but Paco shook his head. He was well known for composing and singing corridos on the spot, but today his grief was too heavy.

"Maybe my primo," he replied, and handed the guitar to his cousin Rudolfo Anaya from Santa Rosa.

"I will try," Rudolfo said, taking the guitar. He thought for a few minutes. "Bueno, 'El Corrido de Billy the Kid' goes something like this":

> Fue una noche oscura y triste
> en el pueblo de Fort Sumner,
> cuando el sheriff Pat Garrett
> a Billy the Kid mató,
> a Billy the Kid mató.
>
> Mil ochocientos ochenta y uno,
> presente lo tengo yo,
> cuando en la casa de Pedro Maxwell
> nomás dos tiros le dio,
> nomás dos tiros le dio.

Vuela, vuela palomita,
a los pueblos del Río Pecos,
cuéntale a las morenitas
que ya su Billy murió,
que ya su Billy murió.

¡Ay, qué cobarde el Pat Garrett,
ni chansa a Billy le dio!
En los brazos de su amada,
ahí mismo lo mató,
ahí mismo lo mató.

Ay, qué tristeza me da
ver a Rosita llorando,
y el pobre Billy en sus brazos,
con su sangre derramando,
con su sangre derramando.

Vuela, vuela palomita,
a los pueblos del Río Pecos,
cuéntale a las morenitas,
que ya su Billy murió,
que ya su Billy murió.*

Paco patted his primo on the back. "Muy bonito" was all he could say, choking with emotion, the same emotion that shook them all. There was nothing left to say.

Each one picked up a handful of earth and tossed it on the coffin. Some of the women threw in the wild sunflowers the children had gathered that morning. Others had come with bright red Rosas de Castilla they had cut from bushes they grew. Flowers for Billy adorned the casket.

---

*For the translation of this song, see the epigraph page at the beginning of the book.

Then came the last goodbye as two of the men picked up shovels and began to fill the grave. The earth of the llano that Billy had loved so well now gathered him to rest. A chapter in the Lincoln County War had come to an end.

26

The following morning, Rosa got up early and put her things in order. It was time to go home.

"You are going," Abrana said.

"Yes. Martín is saddling Mancita."

"Puerto de Luna is far. Martín said he go with you."

"He is kind. So are all of you. But I'll be safe."

"Wait a few days."

"I would like to, but it's best I start now."

Abrana understood. Rosa's grief was as heavy as hers.

Rosa knew that her time living in Billy's history was done. The fateful day had come and gone. Now it was time to go home. She would follow the river north to Puerto de Luna. She remembered what her father had told her: trust the river.

Neighbors gathered to say goodbye. "You can stay with us," Josefa said. "Bilito was your friend. You write his story. We, all his compañeros, we want to hear the story."

Martín came up leading Mancita. "Esta yegua take you many places, she is fine horse." He had tied her saddlebag and backpack to the saddle, along with a small bag of corn for Mancita.

"Gracias, Martín." She looked at her friends. "There *will be* many stories written about Bilito."

"I will write what I know," Paco Anaya said. Rosa nodded. Yes, she had read his account of the tragic night. A true story.

"He was a good boy," Josefa said. "But so much killing in this time. The young men carry guns for protection. Someday maybe peace come to Lincoln. There is room for all. We want to live in peace, but no guns. So many young men dead. Now Bilito."

Her eyes were red from crying. Rosa held her and comforted her, but she knew she could not stay. The Arrow of Time was inexorably moving in her soul. Was dark energy the soul of the universe, or was it gravity, or space-time? It didn't matter. Today they all weighed heavy on her.

"I go with you. You not alone. Long ride to Puerto de Luna."

You can't go with me, thought Rosa. I'm going back to the future. "Thank you, Martín. I'll be okay. Now I must go."

"Yes. It is your destiny," Abrana said. She had wrapped tortillas and slices of cured ham in a towel for Rosa.

"Here fósforos to make fire," Martín said. "And water bag."

"I worry for you," Josefa said, hugging Rosa.

"No te apenes. I'll be fine. After all, I rode with Bilito."

Abrana wiped her eyes. "You are good friend, muy fuerte. We the women have to be strong."

Rosa hugged Abrana's daughters. "Yes. We have to be strong."

Looking into the eyes of the girls brought a new wave of sadness. She knew that within the year the two girls would die of diphtheria. She silently cursed the powers that had brought her into the past, because if she couldn't change it, what good did it do to know the tragedies that lay ahead? She thought she had grown hardened enough by now to the fact that she could change nothing. Yet knowing the two girls were destined to die so young made her heart heavy.

It was best to live in the present and work to make it better. The past was dead. No, the future was conditioned by the past; the future *was* the past. Each person carried the weight of the past in the DNA that had played such an important part in evolution since time immemorial. The past made the present, and it would make the future.

Free will, Rosa thought. Perhaps even that was conditioned by neutrons and electrical particles flowing in the blood and the nervous system. Did Billy have free will? Or did he simply live out a story, a plot written long ago?

Josefa blessed her. "Adiós. May the Virgencita be with you."

Rosa nodded. Yes, the Virgin Mary would guide her. How many times while riding with Billy had she said a silent prayer? "Gracias por todo. You have been family to me."

"And you, hijita."

"Adiós. Cuídate."

"Gracias."

"You come back when you can."

"Yes. Come to visit."

Rosa smiled. Was it possible? Would she ever return? "Maybe," she whispered.

One by one, they stepped forward to hug Rosa and wish her a safe journey.

The July morning was fresh with promise. Later, the llano would bake. At the cemetery, a mound of fresh dirt marked Billy's grave. Like Charlie Bowdre and Tom O'Folliard before him, Billy slept.

Martín handed her Mancita's reins. "You be safe," he said.

"I will," Rosa said.

Paco Anaya stepped up. "Maybe one of the muchachos go with you."

"Gracias, but I will be safe." She stroked the mare's muzzle. "Mancita will take me home." She mounted, and the mare nodded and turned into the road.

"¡Adiós!" Rosa called.

"¡Adiós! ¡Que vayas con Dios!" they called back, and stood watching as she started east toward the river.

She had grown to love them, but she had to leave. Even knowing beforehand the details of Billy's death did not assuage her grief. Billy's friends would know sadness for many years, and the stories they told their children and grandchildren would sadden their hearts. Why did he have to die? they would ask. There was no easy answer. A sad longing for Bilito would spread into the future.

She stopped at the cemetery. A young man named Mireles stood a ways off, strumming a guitar. Rosa listened, then began to sing softly:

> Oh Billy boy, the guitar, the guitar's song is calling.
> From valley to valley and down the mountain side.
> The summer's gone, and all the flowers fading.
> It's you, it's you must go and I must bide.

But please come back when summer's on the llano.
Or when our Pecos Valley is quiet and white with snow.
I'll be there in sunshine or in shadow,
Oh Billy boy, oh Billy boy, I love you so.

But if you come, and all the flowers are dying,
And I am dead, as dead I well may be.
Come and find the place where I am lying,
Kneel and say an "Ave Maria" for me.

And I will feel how soft you walk above me.
Then my grave will warmer, sweeter be.
Bend down and tell me that you love me,
And I will sleep in peace until you come to me.

Eyes full of tears, Rosa turned Mancita, rode till she came to the river, and stopped under a large cottonwood tree. She led the mare down a sandy incline to the water's edge to drink and let her browse on the thick, juicy grasses. The cottonwoods were glistening green, the leaves shimmering in a gentle breeze, the same welcome breeze that cooled Rosa's face.

She sat and contemplated the muddy brown waters. A July flood had gone by a day or two earlier, leaving a lazy flow in its wake. Summer thunderstorms up in the Pecos Mountains, or in the Anton Chico or Santa Rosa area, had turned the tranquil Pecos into a raging river.

Time was like that, sometimes slow and peaceful, other times fast and turbulent. Time and the river came together.

Life is like a river, a guru had pronounced. There was truth in that, Rosa thought. Now the river was gentle. Dozens of carp flapped in the shallows, swimming upriver to the deep pools where they lived. They had been washed down by a flood, and now they were returning home.

A very large one shimmered gold in the light.

"The golden carp," Rosa gasped. The golden carp from a story told by the man who had told Ultima's story. She had seen the boys fishing at the river when they left Puerto de Luna. Now the carp had appeared, a miracle.

She sat mesmerized by the water and the golden sheen on its surface. Sleepy, she closed her eyes. Returning home, going against the current like the carp, going against time. The river contained the history of the people; it was their space-time.

Suddenly she opened her eyes. She cried out, "The river is the wormhole! The river flows from there to here, following the curvature of the earth. The river brought me here! It will take me back!"

The river was a bridge from time present to time past, from time past back to the present! With Billy she had entered the river's energy at the Puerto de Luna Bridge and been transported to Lincoln County. The river connected separate points in space-time! The river was the bridge that had brought her through.

Suddenly it all made sense!

This is why she was following the river back to Puerto de Luna. This was the river of her ancestors. They had tasted its waters and used them to irrigate their crops. Their blood flowed in these waters. Time, the illusion of time, resided in the water and in the land. The river's water was the magic that flowed in her veins. The compass!

She spoke to Mancita. "Wormholes are not only created by exploding supernovas, they're also created by nature here on earth! The river creates a bridge, and so do mountains and deserts and oceans. Nature is the bridge to other dimensions. This is what I learned when I rode with Billy to Lincoln County!"

Let the galaxies spin and expand in their own time; let exploding giant stars create wormholes in dark space. This bridge was made by time and the river. The river was history, ancestors, family, home, fields of corn and chile, patches of squash, apple orchards, fiestas, stories, neighbors sharing, giving, loving, community, and community was a village.

"I am part of all that. I am New Mexican, and New Mexico is my village!" she shouted.

An owl answered from a nearby tree. Was she returning to the time of Ultima? Boys ran, splashing in the river. She heard their joyful shouts. "Hey, Bones, Horse, Tony, Vitamin Kid, Red, Lloyd, Mel, Uli Beri, all the Santa Rosa kids, Ron, JD, Ida, Dolly, Kiko, dead Florence, raaaace!" They were racing across time.

The sounds grew silent. Rosa took a deep, appreciative breath. That story had captured the time of childhood.

Saytir had lied. C-Force did not have a machine that could create wormholes. Wormholes were part of nature, part of the consciousness of the earth. The Mississippi, the Amazon, the Grand Canyon, the Sahara, White Sands, Antarctica, in those places one could let nature's beauty and power transport the soul. Nature was the bridge the soul could use to cross over to new worlds.

"Gracias a Dios," she whispered.

But it wasn't just the grandiose and spectacular potential of a wondrous world that created nature's bridges. Smaller, simpler places in nature were bridges, too. A river like the Pecos was a bridge, but so was a small creek. Bridges were nature's creation. A forest of aspen in the fall, the setting sun, the sound of surf on a beach, a walk in the outdoors. On and on it went. What scientists called wormholes were really nature's bridges.

Our ancestors had known all along that the powers latent in nature were the same as those energies in space-time, gravity, dark matter, shooting stars. Billy knew. The good people of Lincoln County knew. Now the river was all she needed to return home.

Feeling fulfilled, she mounted and rode north, startling deer that had come to drink in the late afternoon. Twilight set in, and owls and other birds began to call in the bosque. Beaver, mice, squirrels, all sorts of creatures moved in the brush. The spirit of the river moved in the dusk. The hand of creation was moving with the oncoming shadows.

La Llorona cried in the deep shadows, her shadow chasing the boys. "Sister!" Rosa called. "Sister! Watch over the boys. See that they don't drown! You did not murder your child. You cry for our people.

La gente have been robbed of so much. The spirit of our community is wounded. That's what happened in Lincoln, and is happening all over the land. Your cry is a cry to awaken the village. A cry to save the children!"

Yes, save LA! Save Chicago! New York, Miami, Denver, Houston! Wherever children are dying of abuse and drugs! La Llorona cried. In the streets of every city across the nation, La Llorona cried for the children.

Save us from a mad president who murders the soul of our village. He turns people against people. He does not see that the children are drowning. La Llorona, this wounded mother, will not be silenced. Her cry echoes across the country: Build bridges, not walls. Save the village.

The revelation strengthened Rosa. She would make new resolutions for the future. With others she would cry out in protest, cry with La Llorona and awaken the people, march with the sisters of the Crying Woman.

Joy filled her heart as she skillfully rode Mancita around quicksand bogs and prairie dog towns where she might trip. Late in the day, she came upon the old sheepherder camp where she and Billy had rested. The ramada would be her shelter for the night. Loosely piled rocks held up the roof of cottonwood branches. It had been a shelter for many a previous wanderer along the river. How many had used the river as a bridge through time?

She fed Mancita the corn Martín had packed. She built a fire and ate the food Abrana had sent. She spread the horse blanket and lay down to rest. The fire died, leaving a few embers and wisps of curling smoke.

Overhead the universe was alive with a million stars, the lights from millions of galaxies. The lights just arriving on earth came from the time of creation. The Big Bang, stargazers called it. Space-time, gravity pulling at every bit of mass, $E = mc^2$, stellar dust and radiation falling into black holes, and the whole enchilada flying away, expanding.

From where, to where?

All that mystery was out there, but it was also in Rosa's heart that night. The heart created a bridge from the lover to the beloved. Love and goodness multiplied. Love squared was the gravity holding the universe together.

Meditation and prayer could create bridges, and so could a church service where the mystery of faith was revealed. All religions praying for peace and reconciliation made bridges. So did a corn dance at Isleta Pueblo, sweet earth after a rainstorm, children playing on a school ground. All these ceremonies created sacred space. Sasquatch would return home on the bridge created by a Mescalero ceremony.

"We can create sacred space!" Rosa whispered. "Our ceremonies create sacred space."

She had felt it one day at Jemez Pueblo. The Matachine dancers had finished for the day. Rosa stepped on the earth where they had danced and felt a power uplifting her, a joy in her heart.

"It was there all along," she whispered and smiled.

The gentle murmur of the river lent its music to the orchestra playing in the stars overhead. Rosa pulled the blanket around her, and lullabied by Ultima's owl, she closed her eyes. The owl watched over her, its soft hoo-hoo guiding her homeward.

Dreams were bridges made of soul power. Rosa sighed and opened her heart to the mystery revealed. She slept.

Billy appeared and spoke in a soft voice. "Darn, Rosa. I'm sure glad you rode with me. It were a go, warn't it." He laughed. "Glad you'll be home safe tomorrow."

27

Rosa crossed the bridge and rode into Puerto de Luna in the late afternoon. Here Coronado had built a bridge over the Pecos River in 1540, so the story went. Now it was her bridge home. Lord, she thought, the footprints of those who have crisscrossed this land are everywhere. But I am home. Gracias a Dios.

From here she could see her casita, the house she had rented for the summer. The small adobe had been perfect for her needs. Beyond that was the church. The village was quiet. A truck passed her, headed toward Santa Rosa. A dog came out from beneath an elm tree, barked once, then went back to the shade.

She reined up in front of Shorty's home. He had just finished watering his small garden by the side of the house. "Hi, Rosa," he called. "How was the ride?"

Startled, Rosa pulled on Mancita's reins. "What?"

"How was the ride?" he asked again.

The ride with Billy the Kid? Is that what he meant? Of course not; he didn't know. What could she say? He thought she had been out for a ride that afternoon. She looked around: nothing had changed.

"Good," was all she could mumble.

"Where'd you get the saddlebag?"

"Josefa—" She stopped short. "A friend."

She waited. She'd been gone for years with Billy, but Shorty meant how was her regular afternoon ride. Time was loosening its grip on her.

"Eloisa's baked pies today. Come in for coffee and pie."

"Maybe later," she managed to say, her mouth as dry as cotton. "I'd better get in."

"Okey-dokey. We'll save you some." He laughed and disappeared into the house.

"Gracias," Rosa whispered.

She rode on to the corral, dismounted, and led Mancita in. She felt dizzy. Like I never left, she thought. Got to touch something real. She patted Mancita. Slowly, as if sensing these things for the first time, she removed the bridle, saddle, saddlebag, and backpack.

The bridle and saddle go in the tack shed, she remembered. That was familiar. And the smell of the corral was familiar, the milk cow Shorty kept, dry manure, a fly buzzing, the sun setting in the west.

She brushed Mancita, enjoying the reality of the touch. "Thank you, "she said and looked around. "Thank you. Thank you."

She thanked the Virgin Mary for bringing her home safe. She hurried into the house and paused at the door to orient herself. Everything was as she had left it. Her manuscript on the desk, the desk lamp still lit, the chairs all in place. "I didn't sleep here last night. The bed is still made."

The owl had lulled her to sleep last night. She was sure she had been at the sheepherder's camp. Thunder had sounded far away. Lightning had flashed over Fort Sumner. Did lightning have any-thing to do with the river bridge? Was lightning a burst of nature's energy that could create bridges to other dimensions? A rainbow was a bridge. All of nature's creations if engaged with faith could take the soul from one time to another.

That was the conclusion she had come to last night, except that there had been no last night. She remembered waking to a gorgeous sunrise, a magnificent palette of colors, the light shining on the cot-tonwoods, spilling across the llano unto the purple hills. The call of birds in the trees, Mancita snorting, eager to be on the way. Familiar sounds and light—she remembered those things.

The Arrow of Time was arcing over the river; the river was flow-ing south. The bridge she had used to get home was real, full of potency, a bridge from there to here. Could she use it to visit heaven and return? The beauty and energy in nature had connected her soul with the spirit in nature. That connection was a bridge. It was the passage of the soul to another time. It was soul passage.

Attentive to the marvelous in nature, the soul could create a bridge to other times, and in that ecstatic moment the soul could be there for a minute or for an eternity. All the saints, gurus, priests, shamans, and those who prayed deeply or did meditation knew this. Was that it, the ecstatic moment? Its gift to humans was as old as Adam and Eve awakening in the Garden of Eden.

She opened her eyes and thanked the light.

Billy was still on her mind. He had appeared in her dream, smiling and cocky, so sure of himself. He was telling her not to worry, the past was past, but in her heart she knew the past would never let her go. What she had been through with Billy was engraved in her heart. "I was there," she insisted. "I have to believe! The Arrow of Time can be conquered."

Now she knew she could bend the Arrow into her story and make time stand still. The story captured time; writing the story created sacred space. The eternal struggle over time had been missing from her story. Now she knew, writing the novel allowed her to live in the creative moment and capture time. All artists knew this. All creators practiced stopping time.

A reader reading her novel could also indulge in time standing still, the singularity of creation. It had been so all along. That's why she wrote stories, that's why she had wanted to write the true story of Billy the Kid. To live fully in the space of creation.

The novel was soul passage, the bridge she was building. She felt the power of creation flowing through her. She heard herself laughing, a long, joyful laugh. "By gosh, Billy, warn't it a ride? It darn sure was!"

Time had delivered Rosa home. Now she knew she could curve the Arrow of Time into the story, into her life. In the act of creation, soul could curve space-time. Soul was stronger than gravity. Soul contained the universe. She would have to learn to live with this newfound knowledge.

What if the notes she had stored on her laptop had been erased? Traveling through space-time was like entering a black hole: once past the event horizon, electromagnetic particles could have changed her story, creating a new one. What would it read like?

She couldn't move. She stood looking into the shadowed room. Not a thing was out of place. Nothing had moved on her desk. Her papers and her books were right where she had left them. The clock was ticking. There had been no day lost.

What then?

She dropped her backpack, placed the saddlebag on the desk, and sat down. She looked out the window. The village was quiet, not a thing moving in the dying afternoon light. She could hear the faint splash of the river behind the house. Gathering her manuscript as a pillow, she laid her head on it.

She had always loved the feel and challenge of paper before it was written on. So fresh and innocent until words were recorded, until soul created the bridge to harness the Arrow of Time. Was this the story she had written or the story she would write? She had lived the story. Now what?

In a while she would call home, talk to her parents, make ordinary conversation: How were they, she was fine, the novel was coming along. She would call Bobby. How was he? How were her students? Was Leonor still off meth? How was the weather? She would no longer communicate with Marcy. That was done. Later, she would go to Eloisa's for home-baked pie.

For the moment, she needed to indulge all her senses in this new reality. See, feel, smell, taste, listen to everything around her. Reorient her soul. She was okay. What had gotten into her was the story she was writing, the river and its mystery, her ancestral blood and the memories it carried, all the things that created soul passage. Her creativity was a bridge over troubled waters. She could make time stand still.

She would honor the years spent with Billy, Josefa and Martín, the Regulators, all the characters in the Lincoln County War. Yes, even Saytir. If she believed Marcy, C-Force would have Saytir sitting in the Oval Office. She had to call the FBI, the newspapers, let everybody know. Get out and join the women's marches. There was so much to do.

She looked at the saddlebag Josefa had given her. How did it get here? She grabbed her backpack, reached in, and emptied the contents. Shoes, shirts, pants, everything scattered on the floor. There, neatly tucked at the bottom, was the blue taffeta dress. She picked it up and smothered her face in it.

For a moment it was all too much. She felt a sob coming up from somewhere very deep. She was crying for Billy. She was crying for herself.

Rosa's Notes and Observations

On September 17 or November 20 or November 23, 1859, depending on the source, Henry McCarty is born to Patrick and Catherine McCarty, probably in Manhattan or Brooklyn. (Is he of Irish heritage?) He has a brother, Joseph. Following Patrick's death, Catherine and her sons move to Indianapolis. There she meets William Henry Harrison "Bill" Antrim.

In 1870, Catherine, the boys, and Bill Antrim are in Wichita, Kansas. From there they move on to Denver in 1871, then to Santa Fe in 1873. Catherine marries Bill Antrim in Santa Fe in 1873, and that same year they move to Silver City. Catherine will die there of tuberculosis in 1874.

It was from his mother that Henry learned to read, sing, and dance.

When Henry is fifteen, he and his friend Sombrero Jack are accused of stealing some laundry. Billy is arrested and locked up to teach him a lesson, but he escapes through the jail chimney and flees to the Arizona Territory, where he works as a ranch hand. It is there that he will learn how to make money by stealing horses.

In 1877, seventeen-year-old Henry is hanging out around Camp Grant near Silver City. In August he shoots and kills a bully named Windy Cahill. Once again he flees, ending up in Lincoln County, New Mexico. The law begins to call him "the Kid."

Henry adopts an alias, William H. Bonney, and thus becomes Billy Bonney. Why did he choose the Bonney surname? Are the roots of the name Irish or French? The Bonney family who settled in the Pastura, New Mexico, area probably arrived via the same route used by many immigrants from the East, following the Santa Fe Trail into the New Mexico Territory. Old-timers said the Bonneys came down to Pastura from the Wagon Mound area.

Ramón Bonney was born in March 1846. He married Anastacia Lucero, who was twenty-four years his junior, born May 21, 1870. A son from this marriage was Juan Salomón Bonney, who was born in May 1893. In the early 1920s, Rudolfo Anaya's mother, Rafaelita (née Mares; born July 26, 1904), was married to Juan Salomón Bonney, who died a few years later. They had two children, Elvira (born February 11, 1924) and Salomón Jr. (born October 30, 1925).

In October 1877, Billy shows up in Lincoln, New Mexico. He is described as weighing 135 pounds, muscular and wiry, with brown hair, clear blue eyes, and buckteeth and wearing a plain Mexican sombrero.

Lincoln, on the Río Bonito, is a village of Anglo-American and Mexican families. The nearby garrison Fort Stanton keeps an eye on the Mescalero Apaches.

New Mexico becomes a territory after the war with Mexico ends in 1848. It will become a state in 1912.

Ethnic tensions exist between many of the homesteading Texans and the Mexicanos. Black soldiers are stationed at the fort. Most hate the Mescalero Apaches.

Henry learned Spanish, probably while living in Santa Fe, which endeared him to the Mexicanos of Lincoln County. These families are no longer citizens of Mexico; they became U.S. citizens after Mexico lost its northern territory to the U.S. after the Mexican-American War of 1846–48. The Treaty of Guadalupe Hidalgo was signed in 1848. All Mexicanos living in prior Mexican territories are now U.S. citizens.

John Chisum arrives in 1867 and runs thousands of cattle on the plains east of the Pecos River. The famous cattle trails these cattlemen are said to have discovered are actually well-known old Comanche trails. The Hispano ciboleros from the Taos and Santa Fe area had used the same trails long before the Goodnights, etc.

In September 1877, Kid Antrim is a member of the notorious Lincoln County gang called "the Boys," which is headed by Jesse Evans.

In 1869, Lawrence Gustave Murphy and Emil Fritz establish a mercantile and banking business, L. G. Murphy & Co., at Fort Stanton. After Fritz dies in 1873, a clerk who has worked for the business, James J. "Jimmy" Dolan, becomes Murphy's new business partner. They control the dry goods and cattle business in Lincoln County and reap the profits of government contracts to sell beef to Fort Stanton and the nearby Mescalero Apache reservation.

John H. Tunstall, an Englishman, arrives in Lincoln in 1877 and teams up with Alexander A. McSween, a lawyer, to compete with the Dolan monopoly. They establish the Lincoln County Bank. They befriend John Chisum.

The Tunstall and Dolan factions will be the opposing "armies" in the Lincoln County War, which will be fought over power and wealth. In 1877 Billy is working for the Murphy clan with his old friend Jesse Evans, who will later become an enemy. Sheriff William J. Brady jails Evans. In November the Boys and Billy break Jesse out of the Lincoln jail.

Billy leaves the gang and meets the Coe family. He later goes to work for John Henry Tunstall, a man he will grow to love as a father. He meets most of the men who will later be known as the Regulators. He enjoys bailes (dances) and the Mexicana girls of the area.

Billy and Fred Waite have plans to buy a ranch, but get caught up in defending McSween's property after Dolan attaches both McSween's and Tunstall's property. Each side begins to issue warrants on the other.

In February 1878, Tom Hill, Jesse Evans, and Billy Morton murder John Tunstall, claiming to be a posse legally charged to be deputy sheriffs. Tunstall's murder sets off the Lincoln County War. Both sides see the conflict as just that, a *war*, and ambushes and murder are the rule.

Billy Bonney, the Kid, vows revenge. He now has a cause. Warrants are issued for Tunstall's killers. It is now McSween vs. Dolan. As to which warrants are *legal*, that will be one of the complex issues of the war.

Also in February, Constable Atanacio Martínez, Billy Bonney, and Fred Waite attempt to serve a warrant on Sheriff Brady. Brady takes them prisoner. A day later he releases Billy and Fred but keeps their weapons. Billy feels humiliated by Brady.

In March 1878, Martínez and Dick Brewer form a posse they call the Regulators, who consider themselves agents of the law. Billy serves in most of their major operations.

Also in March, Billy Morton, in escaping, kills Regulator William McCloskey. The Regulators, with Billy involved, kill Morton and Frank Baker. Dolan says this was murder. Billy has vowed revenge for Tunstall's murder.

Governor Samuel B. Axtell is a friend of U.S. District Attorney Thomas B. Catron; both side with Dolan.

McSween suggests that Brady, who is generally seen as an honest, respected citizen, should be murdered. Brady favors Dolan and has abused Bonney and Waite.

On April 1, Frank McNab, Henry Brown, Jim French, John Middleton, Fred Waite, and Billy Bonney hide in a corral behind the Tunstall store. Brady and four deputies walk to the courthouse. When they are on their way back, the Regulators open fire, killing Brady and George Hindman. Billy rushes to Brady to retrieve his Winchester and is shot in the thigh.

Lincoln is shocked. Public opinion turns against McSween, who agrees to place himself in military custody at Fort Stanton. The U.S. Army headquartered there will off and on play an important role in the Lincoln County War.

The historian Herodotus wrote: "No one is so foolish as to prefer war to peace: in peace children bury their fathers, while in war fathers bury their children."

Later Thucydides wrote: "Men go to war out of honor, fear, and (self) interest." Did the Lincoln County War involve all three?

On April 4, Billy and the Regulators, who have been in San Patricio, are back at Blazer's Mills, where they run into Buckshot Roberts, who was at the ranch when Morton's posse killed Tunstall. The Regulators have a warrant for Buckshot. He kills Brewer and in turn is shot by Bowdre. Billy rushes Buckshot, showing his reckless bravery. John Middleton is wounded but does not die.

On April 18, a grand jury indicts Billy Bonney and Middleton for the murder of Sheriff Brady. Bowdre is charged with murdering Buckshot. John Copeland is the new sheriff and is friendly to the Regulators.

The Dolan posse heads for Lincoln to arrest the killers of Brady, Hindman, and Roberts. "Dutch Charlie" Kruling is killed by George Coe. Strangely enough, he is the only casualty of the Battle of Lincoln. For four hours the Dolan posse exchanges fire with the Regulators, but surprisingly, no one is hurt. In many of the ensuing skirmishes, hundreds of rounds are fired. One would have expected many more dead.

On April 5, 1878, Colonel Nathan Dudley assumes command of Fort Stanton. Doc Scurlock now heads the Regulators and forces Copeland to make him a deputy. Each side claims to be the rightful law.

Mexicano vaqueros led by Josefita Chávez join the Regulators. Little is known of this woman who dared to ride with Billy Bonney's gang.

The Regulators capture Manuel "el Indio" Segovia, and Billy and Josefita kill him when he tries to escape.

The Regulators have taken Thomas B. Catron's horses thinking they were Dolan's. Furious, Catron complains to Governor Axtell.

A federal investigation by Frank Angel begins. Billy gives a deposition. George Peppin is appointed Lincoln County sheriff. Billy is wanted on a territorial warrant for Brady's murder and on a federal warrant for the murder of Buckshot. He flees to San Patricio.

In March, while hiding out at the Chisum ranch, Billy carries on a brief romance with sixteen-year-old Sallie Chisum.

The Battle of Lincoln begins on April 30, 1878, when a Seven Rivers posse (the Dolan posse) exchanges fire with the Regulators. This first clash will be followed by two gunfights, one at San Patricio and one at Chisum Ranch. No one is killed.

Sixteen-year-old Tom O'Folliard from Texas becomes Billy's best friend.

On July 15, Sheriff Peppin's posse rides into Lincoln and is attacked by Regulators at McSween's house. The five-day battle for Lincoln begins. Mexicanos fight on both sides, more with the Regulators. Colonel Dudley marches troops into town. The McSween house is burned to the ground. McSween, Francisco Zamora, and Vicente Romero are gunned down.

Yginio Salazar is shot. Florencio Chávez, José María Sánchez, Ygnacio González, Billy, and others escape to the river. By July 19, the five-day battle for Lincoln is over.

On August 5, the Regulators show up at the South Fork Indian Agency. A battle ensues, and Atanacio Martínez kills clerk Morris Bernstein.

Billy and friends retire to Fort Sumner, where Billy once again courts Sallie Chisum. There is a baile every night. The Hispano/Mexicano girls are complimented for their dancing skills. The Regulators move to Puerto de Luna, then to Anton Chico, again enjoying the bailes, at which Billy is an expert.

In Anton Chico, San Miguel County sheriff Desiderio Romero from Las Vegas confronts the Regulators but backs down. Billy emerges as chief of the Regulators, and they return to Lincoln.

In September and October 1878, Billy and four Regulators are in the Texas Panhandle selling stolen horses. Once this was Kiowa and Comanche country; now the Panhandle is overrun by Texan cattlemen like Charles Goodnight who run large herds on the grassy plain. Billy and Tom return to Fort Sumner, then to Lincoln. The Regulators have broken up.

In October, President Hayes appoints Lew Wallace governor of New Mexico. In November, Wallace extends a "general pardon" to offenders in the Lincoln County War, but he does not include Billy, who is under territorial and federal indictment.

In February 1879, Billy's friends and Dolan's people reach a "peace" agreement. An innocent bystander, Huston Chapman, is killed during the revelry.

On March 15, Governor Wallace visits Lincoln. "Kid Antrim" writes the governor and vows to testify against the Dolan gang for killing Chapman, thus breaking the "peace" agreement.

On March 17, Billy meets Governor Wallace at the home of Squire Wilson. Billy understands that he will receive a full pardon if he testifies against those who murdered Chapman.

On March 21, Billy and Tom O'Folliard are arrested and jailed.

Billy and Tom testify before a grand jury and name Dolan and Campbell as Chapman's murderers, but District Attorney Rynerson is out to get Billy for Brady's murder.

Billy feels betrayed by the governor. He leaves for Las Vegas in June 1879, then returns to Lincoln, now running from both murder charges.

In late 1879, Billy heads for Fort Sumner, where he deals monte at the Beaver Smith saloon. There are many bailes, about the only entertainment the natives can enjoy. Many a young Mexicanita is fascinated by the young Billy, among them Nasaria Yerby, Paulita Maxwell, Manuela, Celsa Gutiérrez, and Abrana García.

From October 1879 to January 1880, Billy is rustling cattle to sell to the U.S. Army, the Mescalero Indian Agency, and the booming gold rush town of White Oaks.

Billy kills a drunken Joe Grant at Hargrove's saloon in Fort Sumner. Billy had moved the cylinder in Grant's pistol so that when he shot at Billy, it fired on empty chambers. The Cahill and Grant killings are the only two that can solely be attributed to Billy.

Texas cattlemen form the Texas and Southwestern Cattle Raisers Association to stop rustling. The U.S. Secret Service sends agent Azariah Wild to investigate counterfeiting of banknotes.

In the summer of 1880, Billy is hanging out in Fort Sumner and at nearby ranches with friends.

On November 2, 1880, Pat Garrett is elected sheriff of Lincoln County. Capturing Billy is high on his list of priorities.

Early in November, a posse surrounds Billy and friends at the Greathouse Ranch. Jimmy Carlyle tries to escape and is killed in an exchange of gunfire. Billy is blamed, but perhaps both parties fired on Carlyle.

On November 29, Garrett and Olinger set out from Roswell with a small posse.

On December 12, Billy writes Governor Wallace that he went to White Oaks to see his attorney, Ira Leonard, and that the posse that surrounded him was out to kill him. They fire at him at Coyote Springs and corner him at the Greathouse Ranch. He escapes on foot. He also blames John Chisum.

On December 15, Governor Wallace no longer feels obligated to Billy and posts a five-hundred-dollar reward for "the Kid." Billy has gained notoriety and become a wanted criminal.

On December 19, at Arroyo Cañaditas near Fort Sumner, Garrett and his posse kill Tom O'Folliard.

In December 1880, an article in the *Las Vegas Gazette* uses the name "Billy the Kid" and charges that he is an outlaw and the leader of over forty thieves. The *New York Sun* runs much the same article.

On December 23, Garrett tracks Billy and friends to Stinking Springs. Charlie Bowdre is killed, and Billy surrenders.

On December 24, Billy and Dave Rudabaugh are taken prisoner, delivered first to Fort Sumner, and then in a wagon to Las Vegas, New Mexico. Charlie Bowdre's body is delivered to his wife.

Garrett's posse and prisoners enjoy Christmas dinner at Padre Polaco's store in Puerto de Luna, then leave for Las Vegas. They arrive on the 26th. Everybody wants to catch a glimpse of Billy.

On December 27, Garrett delivers the prisoners by train to Santa Fe, New Mexico, where they are jailed.

On January 1, 1881, Billy writes Governor Wallace asking for a meeting. The governor is out of town.

On February 28, Billy tries to dig his way out of jail. He is caught and chained to the floor in a solitary cell.

On March 2, Billy writes the governor again, but receives no reply. He writes again two days later.

On March 27, he writes yet again, and yet again is ignored. What archive (library) holds these letters?

On March 28, Billy is transported to Mesilla, New Mexico (near Las Cruces), for trial.

On March 30, the first trial for the killing of Buckshot Roberts begins.

On April 6, the case is dismissed. The reasons for this have not been found.

On April 8, the trial for the killing of Sheriff Brady begins.

On April 9, Billy is found guilty of first-degree murder and given the death penalty. (Remember, of all the men killed during the Lincoln County War, Billy is the only one convicted. The others who were tried were acquitted or pardoned. Was justice served?)

On April 13, Billy is sentenced to be hanged on May 13 between 9 A.M. and 3 P.M.

On April 15, Billy writes to Rudabaugh's attorney, Edgar Caypless, asking for help in getting his mare back so he can sell her and pay his own attorney, Albert Fountain, but Caypless is unable to help. Fountain's future becomes a New Mexico murder case, unsolved. Billy is transported to Lincoln.

On April 21, Billy arrives at Lincoln and is jailed at the courthouse.

On April 28, he kills two guards and escapes. The Great Escape is the theme of many movies and is reenacted in Lincoln every year as a tourist attraction.

July 14, 1881, is the fateful day. Billy is shot and killed by Garrett in Pete Maxwell's house. He was twenty-one. Was he ambushed? What role did Maxwell play?

On July 15, Milnor Rudulph organizes a coroner's jury, which finds that Billy's death was justifiable homicide. Garrett can collect the reward money. Billy is buried next to his good friends Charlie Bowdre and Tom O'Folliard in the military cemetery at Fort Sumner. (But are they really buried there?)

In 1882, Garrett writes *The Authentic Life of Billy the Kid*. More myth than fact, it remains the most read book about Billy. And so with

---

this book the legend of Billy the Kid grows and grows. Paco Anaya's book, *I Buried Billy*, is a true account but not very well known.

What do you think? Do we really know the true Billy? Or are we satisfied with the legend, the bits and pieces of his life?

Bless Me, Ultima
Heart of Aztlan
Tortuga
The Silence of the Llano
The Legend of La Llorona
The Adventures of Juan Chicaspatas
A Chicano in China
Lord of the Dawn: The Legend of Quetzalcóatl
Alburquerque
The Anaya Reader
Zia Summer
Jalamanta: A Message from the Desert
Rio Grande Fall
Shaman Winter
Serafina's Stories
Jemez Spring
Curse of the ChupaCabra
The Man Who Could Fly and Other Stories
ChupaCabra and the Roswell UFO
The Essays
Randy Lopez Goes Home
Billy the Kid and Other Plays
The Old Man's Love Story
Poems from the Río Grande
Isis in the Heart
The Sorrows of Young Alfonso